# In the

# Company of

# Women

JONATHAN LOVEJOY

Armageddon Publishing
All rights reserved.

Cover: *The Penitent* 1876
William Adolphe Bouguereau (1825-1905)

ISBN-10: 069294486
ISBN-13: 978-0692394489

*For every Jeannie*

*And I saw the woman drunken with the blood of the saints...*

Revelation 17:6

*Jonathan Lovejoy*

# Mothers and Daughters

$\mathcal{V}$ampires are not created. They are born.

Forget everything you've ever read about vampires. It's all bullshit. We can't fly. We're not immortal. But what we do have… is power. The power of charm. The power of charisma. The ability to make other people trust us. To like us. We do it without effort. By natural instinct. The way that a Cheetah runs 70 miles per hour on the open plains. For survival.

It is impossible not to like us. To be attracted to us. And though my lover and I are both women, the blood of a woman is paramount. Mothers and daughters. Women and girls. The blood of another

woman is sweet to the taste. It nourishes our bodies—for Christ's sake. Amen.

The music of their screams is milk for the soul. Her desperation is like wine. Her fear of death is meat for our spirit. To lure some unsuspecting little self-pleased, self righteous, self absorbed, self aggrandizing little bitch into our home—to watch the look of shock come over her face. To feel the terror take over her body. The smell of a woman's fear is a pheromone to our libido. It is like the smell of a steakhouse grill on a hungry Friday night.

For Anya and me, the sound of this corporate bitch's screams feeds us from head to toe, as she lies underneath us in a deep, woman's scream of angry fear. A scream of desperation.

A death scream.

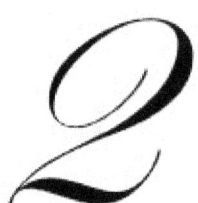

All legends have their basis in fact. Dragons. Bigfoot. UFO's. Ghosts. Werewolves.

And us.

Lore of vampire flight is based on what unnatural strength, speed and agility we do possess. It goes back to the question of survival again. We can get to a victim from the other side of a room at the moment they think they are about to escape out the door. But this isn't the way it happened with Miss Corporate Forty Five here. Twelve years older than the both of us, twelve pounds heavier in the breasts (for Anya, at least), and so too in the hips as well. I guess that's why we were so calm and so quiet with her corporate

loveliness, making her disrobe to her big bra and tight underwear in our soundproof basement room. When it happens in our suburban home, this is where we have to take them, so we're free to listen to them scream.

And this voluptuous, upper middle class queen hath raised the girl cock inside me, honey. Believe me. And I'm proud to admit that this is not figurative, for one of my gifts is that when I am aroused, my two inch clit nearly *triples* in size, enough that I may engage in full woman to woman intercourse—and this, without the toys of legend, which we ladies must sometimes wear as that which pertaineth to a man. My orgasms from this grip my body and beyond, down to the core of my spirit—to make me think only of the Almighty God himself, and to feel as though I may faint into the dizzying haze around me.

And oftentimes my womanhood, the spirit of Woman that lives in me takes over, and I am overwhelmed to weeping. Yes. A weeping orgasm is a reality for some women, and sometimes, most profoundly for me. Often, Anya's strong, merciless aggression is the setup for myself, for the thing that I must do to a victim before she dies—as I watch her break the bonds of cultured civility for me— sometimes physically pummeling a girl or a woman, where I feel my lady cock growing in my Fruit of the Loom or Hanes lady undies

below. Between the two of us, Anya is the physical aggressor, the emotional antagonist, the lioness so much more openly out for the kill. Oh, how many times have I listened to a girl or a woman screaming from bent or broken fingers lying underneath us—this, usually when she is any way resistant, no, in any way a *bitch* to us, which will make her dying that much harder and more painful to endure.

And yes, as it is tonight, as it has always been, this death is not achieved until there is the shedding of blood, until the deep sucking and biting of the neck is done. And of every vampire lore and legend that must be, I am afraid that this one must move from fantasy into reality—yes, our eyes *do* lighten severely from the power that courses through our veins, and the natural mechanism of our canines *does* extend them down just far enough to cause unholy terror in the souls of the eyes that stare.

When our bodies are ready for food, when our spirits are ready to receive the magic of what we do, our faces undergo such a powerful transformation, to where what femininity or appeal we have is enhanced to another level, and we appear at that moment as creatures of the night, though not in the bloody gruesomeness of movies or television, but from what I've seen from Anya, is an almost angelic *beauty*, and aesthetic power unachievable by a normal female. This part of vampire lore and legend, they did get right, I suppose, but I wonder who in the history of man, from the Moors of Scotland to the

foggy countryside of Great Britain, who hath seen one of us at the moment of death, then escaped to live and tell the tale?

Ah, but this woman that lies on the basement bed underneath us, reduced to begging now, intermittent through hopeless and helpless screams, she can only stare in wide eyed disbelief at what she sees pressing down on her from above, the faces of two avenging angels of no mercy, with blue eyes lightened to the color of an arctic sky in winter.

# 3

Once at the turn of every season, we must feed. Otherwise, we descend into madness, until we die. Whether or not this is true for all of us, I do not know. I only know of what stories there are in my own family tree, of what happened to my mother's mother when I was nine. Iris Greenwood (my namesake, though I am called Jeannie, from my name Iris Jean)—Iris lived on the blood of little girls, and that of those that aspired to the age of 16, until eventually her luck ran out. Smart enough to have set herself up in small town elementary school heaven, eventually moving up to Jr. High—to network among the 13 and 14 year old buffet line—just to be near

them when they get off the bus in the morning, when they came into the classroom fresh off another night's sleep, buried in false hope for the future.

Iris Dove Greenwood had worked her way up the ladder from the sixth grade all the way to the eighth, where she could be in the middle of the madness of her world, which was the fungalooga smiles and silliness of mothers and daughters, the smell and scent of their self entitlement and hypocrisy—the secret mother-daughter competition that plagued the smartest and most attractive among them. Always a predator on the prowl for prey, she was, only how different was Iris than every other mother deep within? To her, they all stank of self-righteous superiority and struggle—but this is the struggle for social dominance, the struggle to appear better than their rivals and counterparts—driving and pushing their daughters into this dance class or this gymnastic program or that path to grades and academic glory, and Miss Greenwood being the ringmaster, the eighth grade gatekeeper to young girl paradise—which was all girl trips and girl scout trips and gymnastic trips and cheerleader trips and academic trips and women's museum trips and women's college basketball trips and alcohol trips and secret trips to neighboring towns that nobody knew about except me, while girls anywhere from the age of nine to sixteen might turn up missing forever. And this, she did at least once a year for over 30 years of her life, accumulating at least this many victims across Virginia, North and

South Carolina—until one day, ironically, her undoing came from something that had nothing to do with the killings she had made.

Only 39 victims, one may ask? What of her need to feed four times a year? Why not over one hundred victims? But how practical is that, pray tell, how possible is that? And what of animal blood? Couldn't she have simply gotten a farm and fed on the blood of pigs and cows and chickens, and been in a blood stupor from here to eternity? Iris learned over the years, that some victims must not just be done away with and left in the woods to rot away to bones and nothing else, before every drop of blood in their bodies was drained and stored in her basement deep freezer—bagged, dated and hidden under a panel beneath the frozen strawberries and blueberries that would never be eaten.

And I was nine, when the spirit of Iris' blood came into me. Yes, I was nine, when the spirit of Iris Greenwood hath come.

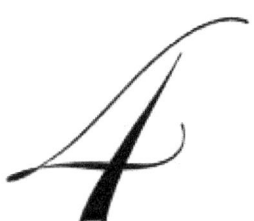

ing dong, the bitch is dead. Sing it high, sing it low. Ding dong the wicked bitch is dead. She's gone where the goblins go below. Below below yo ho. Let's open up and sing. And ring the bells out. Ding dong the bitch is dead. Sing it high. Sing it low. Let them know, the wicked bitch is dead. And her fifty year old blood was red, by which our souls were fed.

Both of us lie here, on top of this dead corporate queen, our bellies full from the blood we drank so hungrily from her neck. And this was something that neither of us could have stopped if we had tried, knowing that her curviness, her hypocrisy, her phoniness and self-righteous repression was going to have to be dealt with sooner or later—but if not by us, then who? What energies would have coalesced and flowed into her life anyway, to vex her with negativity from the clear blue, to make her wish she had never been born? Would it have come from her husband of 30 years, Mr. Blue Collar Fix It, with his successful contracting business, million dollar aspirations always overhead in rainbow form, held out as a promise of false hope that Fate is not obliged to keep? What negativities was this corporate bitch ripe for anyway, having spent her life arguing with and clashing heads like mountain rams with her ambitious 30 year old daughter, job hopping in high heels and business suits from one office job to the next, masters degree and Mama's curves firmly in hand? What is the next comeuppance that is overdue? For none of us will escape judgment, I suppose, and as to where and when it will happen to each of us is a mystery.

For a lifetime of spiritual debauchery, for a generation of worldly ambition, for a daughter raised under the wooden paddle in secret, for the breasts exposed and wobbled behind closed doors while the paddling wood was flown, this woman has seen her last days on earth come and go—this judgment meted out to her early, for God knows already who will accept him and who will not—and this witch's soul was already condemned to Hell. So why wait? Yes. We were the angels of her impending rise and fall—the rise of unearthly

terror in her soul, and the fall of life and breath from her physical body.

*Did you cum,* are the words that flow from me on their own, over the dead body of Barbara Ann Bridgeman, mother of Dianne Bridgeman herself—these words spoken warm into the air, to help me find my way back to twisted sanity.

"You know I did," Anya says. "Twice."

Breathless words spoken, from lips red with ambition, a mouth painted red with a woman's dark destiny fulfilled. Ms. Barbara Ann Bridgeman. Perhaps our latest and greatest victim, a woman whose lifestyle and privilege should have protected her from such a fearful and gruesome death. Wherein she lies cold underneath us, soon to be lying cold and stinking in the earth.

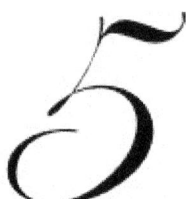

estview Garden Terrace is our half million dollar neighborhood in Richmond, where those who have been privileged enough to be chosen by God rest in lower million dollar luxury, so easily accomplished and achieved by high class salaries and saving and pseudo-money spent through credit. The brick mini-mansion where Anya and I hide from the world is bought and paid for by pure privilege and pre-ordination, by way of a half million dollar trust set up by my grandmother before she died, which I inherited when I was 21. Besides this was the contents of her attic and basement, in the house where my mother decided to live as a bloated breasted

recluse—the isolated, two story farmhouse of legend, somewhere in the farmlands of Virginia, where Elizabeth Greenwood, or Betty Greenwood still lives to this day. A full goth recluse, she is—the fair skin, the height, the beauty, the disdain for people and their bullshit I must have inherited, that sometimes plagues me into a depression. Even while my blonde baby and me drag this dead bitch's corpse through the fall of a fervent summer's night, through the grassy field, to the suburban woods beyond, my heart and mind are drawn to the wicked queen cliché which is my own mother, resting so calm and quiet within herself, wondering where it is that her beloved daughter could have gone.

I am home, Betty Greenwood, obeying the blood that passed through you from Iris, but did not put the lust for human blood in your body. Only the traces of it were passed into thee, Mother Dear—the extreme erotic sensitivity in your body, in particular your breasts—the taste for the sweat and spit of another woman, the need to introduce me to what your mother Iris introduced you to when I was but a girl of twelve. And what need do you hardly have for cookies, cakes and pies, Mother, when your bodies' craving is for the meat and blood of animals—where the rarest steak imaginable is the lust for your craving?

And do you prefer the night to the day, Mother, to drift as a spirit in the time after sunset, as the earth turns again toward the evening day? When you look at the stars that flicker in the twilight—from whence cometh forth the one where your Redemption draweth nigh?

This same bright and evening star, where Anya, Barbara Ann and me ate charred meat and drank the blood of the grape, in the feeling of such hope and promise for the future. She was here to offer Anya Shier, a.k.a. Anya Greenwood (Yes, she is my legal wife), a corporate position from the Barnes and Noble branch she manages, this same one where I was recently made assistant manager. A lesbian married couple, I suppose, lights the fire in the corporate literary mind, in the corporate literary loin, and Barbara Bridgeman suddenly developed a lust to see Anya in one of the highbacked leather chairs in a boardroom beside her. "Mrs." Greenwood. But where is your Mr? This, inside the body of another Mrs, where the name Iris serves as king to her queen.

A lesbian married couple. So modern. So politically correct. So good for the company's public image. *"A lesbian married couple manages one of our Virginia branches,"* has already swept through the company like a wildfire whisper, and one look at Anya Greenwood's body and blonde hair is icing on the Nordic cake—this blue eyed, blonde haired Russian descendent, whose essence is as the frozen Tundra of her ancestry, which is the breathtaking beauty of the vast, open countryside, where the snows cover the ground in pristine white, and the blue sky touches the ground to every horizon.

And so Anya, my love, my heart grieves for thee, as we gather together under these bright, late night summer stars, to stroll

unawares through our dark destiny, lost somewhere in Love's Humility.

My breasts ache—in the tight white T-shirt with no bra, they wobble and shake. Jiggling as I shovel the loose earth into the five and a half foot grave where this bitch is buried. As Anya spits into the grave where she just pissed and shat, saying "good riddance you corporate cunt,"—my breasts wiggle in the memory of tilling the garden soil on the grounds of my youth, which was a farm, no doubt, but only by proximity and appearance, no doubt. The great cornfields that stretched to the woods in the distance were planted by someone else, who rented the land from our enterprising grandmother, and then my mother after Iris was gone. The flip side of generational curses are generational blessings—this, for us, is luck

with lower million dollar money, so that it seems our net worth is always just above seven figures, even without high powered salaries to boot. My grandmother was a genius at saving money, with a talent for investing besides, and her liquidated stocks netted us 1.2 million dollars before she died. Add to this, a trunk filled with gold coins found in the attic which no one ever knew existed, coins worth two and a half million at least, and a life insurance policy worth a million and you get the picture. Iris left us very well off when she passed— thankfully, having the premonition to liquidate her assets into my and my mother's names only a few months before it all ended, lest every penny she had may have been frozen by the authorities when she was caught, arrested, tried, convicted, imprisoned, institutionalized, and buried (though I wanted to say, "interred").

Yes, my breasts ache. They ache with an itchin' slitched by the bitch we bury, and with the memory of Iris and Elizabeth, of the sickness my grandmother passed down to my mother and me. The size and heavy weight of them pulls me into the Heart of Memory, as I shovel the loose earth into this woman's grave, back to when I was but a little girl on the isolated Virginia Farm, just three years after my grandmother had died. I can remember how Betty laid waste to pretense one Friday night when her work was done as the local high school librarian—a job she was more then called to be. Mother was the classic librarian of legend and lore—yes, such women among us do exist as teachers and even the classic image of the beautiful,

repressed librarian, of the kind that makes the groin ache when you see them.

I can vividly recall the tight gray skirts and white blouses and gray sweaters hiding the huge curves she bore, and even the pinned up hair that she never wore in a bun, and the glasses that only enhanced the beauty that she tried to hide. And there was no need for her to *not* wear makeup, because it made no difference whatsoever. Betty Greenwood was a young Joan Collins level beauty at least—with an unearthly sensuality besides, and a body curved into a small waist and big, wide hips of Lopez Land, and breasts as big and heavy as Queen Milena of Velba. How many students and teachers and men and women over the years endured the fire inside from my mother, how many high school boys who didn't even read come to the library just to get a look at what Miss Greenwood was wearing, to see if the top of her blouse would be open or not, to see if she was wearing a loose blouse or not, a loose sweater or not, or a vest or not, or God forbid a blazer jacket or not, but always, everyone in the school was aware of Harland Zachary High School's librarian—the beautiful woman whose breasts were too big and whose butt was too wide and who was too tall and too quiet and too scary to look at and talk to.

Miss Greenwood was intimidating beyond the reason of man and womankind. Yet whenever the barrier was breached, when someone just had to reach out and say something to her about the books or the computers or the records or the classical DVD's, her disarming smile and genuine humility always put them at ease. In the heart of memory, I can see the beautiful woman in the school library, smiling

in a shyness hardly understood, wearing her glasses that she does not need, walking behind the pushcart of books to put back on the shelves, big breasts hung down inside the gray sweater vest, trying so hopelessly, to stay hidden from view. I can see the beautiful, shy, voluptuous image—the classic, cliché of a woman's face and body on the rolling steps, reaching up to re-shelf the books, her bottom widened and rounded in the gray skirt, to cause every man and woman to envy in lust and fear.

I can see the skinny, short haired young teacher who comes into the library often, the light skinned young pretty who comes in to talk to Mother all the time; smiling, laughing, touching her arm, boiling in a lust inside that carries her home on winds of desire at 5:00 every afternoon. Miss Greenwood, she imagines. *Betty Greenwood*, she sketches on her art notebooks at home, of a topless, heavy breasted woman in the library holding a book in nonchalance, casually looking for its rightful place back on the shelf. But alas, skinny-pretty wannabe, those breasts are not yours to fondle, or to shake, to wobble or to suck! This privilege belonged to her mother when she was alive. And now, when I am twelve, the privilege belongs to me.

On this Friday night I so vividly remember, when the blood of her ancestors is resurrected, and the desire coursing through her veins is too much to bear. And this Friday I so vividly recall, perhaps because it is my birthday, and Betty has just brought me home from shopping and a restaurant dinner. She tells me that there is one more

present that she has to give to me tonight, but that it is upstairs in her bedroom.

*"You're such a little beauty,"* she says to me, as we walk up the farmhouse gothic, up the wooden staircase and darkwood banister, my mother's hand so firmly and lovingly at the small of my twelve year old back, giving me a rough, moaning kiss at my temple, that slightly unnerves me. I must admit, wondering what is the source of it—whether it be good for me, or whether it be evil. But good and evil here are separated in my twelve year old mind by punishment and reward, and the fears and nervousness I feel are but the naiveté of a child, on the edge of the Death of Innocence—where there is only the Autumn of the White Woods, and the requisite falling of the forest leaf canopy to the ground.

Through this unmeasured drifting of every wayward leaf, plucked and fallen by winds of what is meant to be, I drift upward through these lusts and wayward desires, the so-called free will of mothers and daughters gone awry, such pleasantness and sweetness arisen from achings that run so far and deep, drifting up the stairs with my mother toward her bedroom rather than mine, where this last and greatest present of my twelfth birthday awaits.

$\mathcal{U}$p the stairs and around the corner we flow, across the threshold of her upper room. Then she takes one hand in mine, and with the other hand she closes the door. As to whether or not I feel imprisoned by her, this, I do not know. Is it freedom or incarceration that flows through my spirit, as the beautiful and statuesque woman escorts me to the side of her bed, and sits down in front of me? *"This is a very special gift,"* she says, her breath tickling my lips, her thumbs brushing across the front of both sides of my dress. Of the depth of feeling, of what infinity of emotion it

flares in my body, of this, I do not know. *"I want you to kiss me,"* Mother says, in such deep and breathy repose, so that I understand that it is not so much a suggestion, as much as it is a high command. And I lean only the slightest bit forward as is required to touch her lips in 12 year old naiveté, eyes wide open to watch hers, feeling the ignition of this fire in my body, as this slightest kiss is already enough to marry the brushing of her thumbs across my breasts hidden under my dress, to give life to the new blue and black fires within. *"Kiss me again,"* she says, but with a greater dominance, so that I know even moreso the nature of this, that this gift is not fun and games, nor is it meant to be trivial in any way, form or fashion. I press my lips to mother's lips again, but this time, unable to pull back, as she puts her hand firmly behind my head and holds it there, as she begins to take over in the wake of her calling, as her kiss suddenly engages mine, in a manner unlike anything I have felt before.

O, Elizabeth! From whence cometh forth this kiss I feel! Which softens your voluptuous lips upon mine, to make the breath flutter inside my body! Kiss me, O kiss me so good, Mother Dear, to relieve the suffering you have caused in my body and soul! And as if to answer my inner craving, the nourishment I feel, she shifts herself forward toward me while still sitting on the edge of the bed, holding the back of my head tighter with me standing there, fully engaging my twelve year old mind and body in the deepest and most sensual

kiss imaginable. As to the feeling which permeates me to the core, of this, I do not know. I only know that the taste of my mother's kiss is sweet, and the feel of her body is meat for my soul. And this, mother endures until she can bear no more, saying to me—*"take off your clothes,"* which I do, lips tucked in shame and humility while she watches me. And I notice though I am ashamed, I am unable to lower my eyes without glancing at her every so often, to see what manner of energy this is that has gripped us, that flows through her and into me, and into the very air we breathe. And it seems that I instinctively know, *not* to stop at my little T-shirt and underwear underneath, taking it off to expose the little piece of fabric that dares inhabit space as a so-called bra, then reaching back to unlatch it, feeling the chill of the darkn'd room at my exposed nipples as well.

Then I stand nude. Naked as the day I was born, while the beautiful librarian stares at me from head to toe, admiring me as a piece of art, seeming to evaluate and access me in a spirit of great curiosity and awe, until the instinct she feels slips the shoes from her feet and bears her up, tall and strong in front of me. *Undo my blouse,* she says, standing in infinite patience and restraint as I fumble with every button until they are done, not sure if I should continue when I reach the front of her tight skirt. *"You can take it off,"* she says, *"all the way."* And this, I proceed to do, pulling it down from her white shoulders until her arms are free, then clumsily yanking and pulling until it is pulled free from her tight skirt, with her standing patiently,

watching to see what I will do with it, whether I will hold it, fold it, or boldly drop it in a heap to the floor.

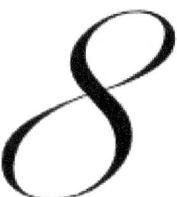

*I*n the Heart of Memory, over the woods high above what it is we do, I see rising above the trees of life, the curvature of the earth as seenfrom outer space. I see my mother's body in the skirt and her bare midriff, arms and mountainous cleavage, her gigantic breasts lifted mightily by the huge, industrial strength bra, which rounds them like the curvature of the earth itself. *"I want you to lift the front of my bra up,"* she says. *"Take the bottom...carefully, now lift up...harder... that's it...slide it up, up..."* And this, I do. Hardly able to lift the heavy weight of my mother's breasts in tow, as I struggle mightily against hope, my feeble young hands gripping the bottom of the bra so tight—sliding the bra up, up, upward, until it seems that Mother's face will be buried in her own cleavage, to suffocate her own depravity to ruin. And I grip and push and pull

against hope, with no help from her on this last, mighty lunge upward, where the bra slips suddenly up and away from her breasts, causing the flop and wobble noisily back down, flapping skin once at where they now rest in perfect beauty, beneath the bra fabric pulled up and away from them. And I notice that when this happens, the pre-ecstasy upon her expression, the look of underlying pleasure on her face is enough to wrinkle her brow and close her eyes, and press her lovely lips into a frown.

*"Now take my bra off,"* she says, telling me to take the back of it in my hands and unhook it, which I do. And once again, she stands there, Unhelpful to my Helpless, waiting to see what her naked daughter is going to do with such a big and beautiful thing as what had held her heavy flesh in tow. With the same pitiful, tuck lipped demurity (or is it shame?), I halfheartedly fold the great fabric and drop it casually to the floor, somewhere near the shoes abandoned, and the white blouse so conspicuously inconspicuous and forgotten.

*"Take it in your hands,"* she says, placing her own hands behind her back as I touch them, causing me to perceive the shudder that twitches her body. *"Now lift them up,"* she says, her voice an octave deeper at least, as I push them up as high as I can. *"Now let them go,"* she says pitifully, as if the words have life of their own accord, as though hardly a power in nature could have prevented them. I let the two great breasts drop, causing her to grunt in this new, deeper voice.

*"Again,"* she says, this time in a sinister whisper, as though she has tasted the forbidden, and now the craving in her body is triggered well beyond the point of no return. This, I do. Lifting them a second

time and letting them drop, bringing a louder grunt from her and a brief shaking of her head 'no,' as if the sensation is as unbelievable as the sight of her own twelve year old daughter unclothed, holding her gigantic breasts up in her tiny hands.

*"Now hold them up,"* she says, nearly losing her breath. *"Hold them still for me."* This, I do. Holding the great, heavy things there, watching her hold her head back in deep rapture and concentration, her chest rising and falling under the full and deep breaths she must take. *"Squeeze them for me,"* she says. Looking down at my clumsiness, delighted by it as I attempt to mash and push and squeeze these to please her anew, looking up at her look down at them, her expression contorted by awe and disbelief.

*"Grab the nipples,"* she says, *"shake them back and forth."* This, I do. Hearing her exclaim to God as her own, breathing, grunting again so long and deep from what to me might seem so naturally benign, and unable to cause such profound pleasures as what she feels. *"Take off my skirt,"* she says, the frustration now a heavy burden on her beautiful features, as she watches me unzip the tight gray skirt and slide it down and away, followed by the sheer black stockings done one at a time, to where I perceive her body's phantom twitching once again. *"Let the underwear stay,"* she says, the white cloth stretched helplessly over the full, widened hips and upper thigh, lost to conceal the impossibly hourglassed and rounded fullness of them.

Elizabeth Elswick—Betty Greenwood's figure is rare among women indeed, meant to remain concealed from what curious eyes that stare, lest it cause a lust and desire unrequited for all time. From the front, the side or the rear, there is only a *woman's* shape to appear, all breasts and hips galore, with a fit, deeply curved waist of such perfect fleshiness as to cause the mouth to water. This deep, inward curve flows outward to these un-casual hips, this unbelievable hip spread to womanliness, to make her a wonder among women to be sure, that such a heavy breasted woman can have such full and fully widened buttocks besides. And unclothed, covered only by the white underwear fabric, the affect is fully Amazonian, where there is only beauty and power, and the strength of unbridled female sensuality. Oh, what casual death could she deliver to another who was bound and gagged, as she smothered them to death with one of her heavy breasts to bear!

*"Pick up a stocking,"* she says. *"Tie it to my wrist, like you're tying a shoe."* This, I do. As she holds her wrist out front to me facing up, I make the first tie. Then she puts her hands behind her back—the other wrist over where the stocking is tied. Then I make another tie—binding the second wrist to the first one. *"Good and tight,"* she says, staring off somewhere beyond the walls, to an unknown place beyond her memory, to where she can feel the spirit of Iris, and what manner of things that were done when she was a little girl herself, and Iris was the tall and fearful woman of beauty.

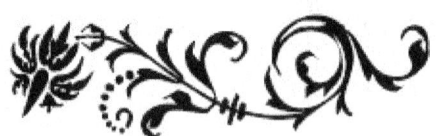

*"Take the other stocking,"* she says. *"Tie it around my thighs, just above the knee."* This, I do. Hearing the breath in her tremble in the quiet of the upper room. Watching the black stocking contrast with the white, fleshy thighs, pressed so tightly together now by the ties that bind, by those that bind the generations together through time. These are the sins of the motherline, those that go undiscussed by all of man and womankind, and remain forever hidden from public view, until the end of the age, when they will be uncovered as a sign unto them, to behold the eve of eschatology, and the rising wind of the Second Coming.

And I look up at the tall and beautiful woman as I tie, who does not look down as she stands with her eyes closed, face anguished over with expectation until I am done. When the stocking is tied around her legs above the knee, I stand in front of her, hardly able to look her in the eye, as she stares at me in utter confidence and control, though her legs and wrists are bound.

*"Take one up in both hands,"* she says. *"Kiss the nipple gently."* This, I do. Holding one of the Great Breasts up with both hands, kissing the white of her breasts and the areola around it, so afraid to kiss the actual nipple, which is nearly flattened, only slightly raised above the rest of her skin. *"Please,"* she says. *"Kiss it."* This, I do. Beginning to finally, timidly kiss on top of the nipple itself, which makes her whole body twitch a shudder. I gently kiss it over and over, listening to her moan pitifully, as if the sensation were somehow the source of a mild, phantom pain somewhere deep

inside. And I notice a mighty shrinking of the big, brown areola occur, and the nipple which was flattened only a moment ago is suddenly twice as high, which beckons me to instinct, and I take it into my mouth in a brief sucking, looking up at her for approval or disapproval, watching her exclaim the name God with force and intrepidity.

And this instinct of mine rings through my mouth, across my tongue to the back of my throat, causing me to pull sharply upward on the nipple, repeatedly, releasing it over and over in a loud sucking, popping sound, until the size of it is magnificent, truly as big as the sweetness of a grape. And this pulling, popping motion soon gives its rightful place to 12 year old instinct, morphed into an outright nursing, which holds her body immobile, her brow wrinkled and mouth open, flowing the sound of an inner weeping from somewhere deep inside her. And I know to at last have mercy on the other side of her being, and I move over to the other nipple and take it quickly into my mouth to a deep nursing, which brings a deep, breathy grunting from her, and a quick powerful shudder from her body. The nursing of this one brings a loud, forceful bellowing from her, a primitive, animalistic noise of private, sensual suffering, of a kind not known to most women, but still understood by the majority of them.

And when she can take no more of her body's Plateau, the painful balancing at the edge, the so-called Precipice of Deluge, she pulls her body up and away, telling me *"take both nipples in your hands."* This, I do. Using the thumb and my forefinger as she has told, as she has begged, twirling and tweaking both nipples and areolas at once, engaging her in the Milk Maiden's Intercourse, which is the pleasure of the breasts by hands and fingers alone, holding both gigantic breasts in both hands, twisting, twirling and tweaking the nipples as she stands with her wrists bound behind her back, bent slightly over in an inner rhythm, her face burdened by a concentration for the ages, until I see that concentration break into a look of profound awe, her eyes still closed, as she bends all the way over and begins to wail a weeping sound from deep within, which then gives way to a series of deep, powerful grunts, which seem to tremble her entire body like an earthquake on the eve of Armageddon.

# In the Haze of a Slow Motion Dream

# 9

 know a mother fucker when I see one. I can smell her coming a mile away. These are not the roots of vulgar slang, which reach down into the corrupted ground, past the corpses and buried secrets and atrocities. No. These are the heights of cultured civility, the branches of public hypocrisy and well-adjusted nonsense. The modern MILFs and MILFettes that stroll through life unseen, unnoticed and undiscovered by everyone they meet. The female teachers, with the lust in their hearts for the shapely little post elementary and pre high school girls, so many of them having tasted their own daughter's skin back when the girls were 13 or so, or perhaps 15—a secret that serves as an invisible glue for this mother

daughter pair. But who among them are the prisoners of this end of the world secret we share? It is an inner sense that all females of my kind possess, being prisoners of this lust ourselves, that the so-called "Mom" in her hip hugging jeans, skin tight T-shirt and beauty salon hair out and styled down past her shoulders, is both a victim and a perpetrator, having been touched by it when she was little, either by her mother or grandmother (aunt or babysitter notwithstanding), becoming acquainted with this power at an early age, giving them special charge over their sexuality from early on—a condition they carry throughout their teenage years and into their adulthood, hiding this deep, otherworldly lust in heterosexuality and suburban Momness to a fault, so that none can sense the Amazonian blood that flows in their veins, that has laid them on top of their daughters in the name of discipline or delight, until they are done listening to the little girls laugh or cry.

I can see it on these women as if they are wearing a sign—they may as well be made of glass, where the walls of secret are transparent to me, and they are hiding nothing of their intentions born in the shadows. Having spent so many years ringing the Barnes and Noble book registers for them, spotting them when they walk in, seeing the aura of it out of the corner of my eye—the seed of which is planted and nurtured in the mother, who, more often than not, is deeply in charge of her womanhood, and is secretly obsessed with what she sees in the mirror. How many of these horny bitches have I seen walk in over the years, sometimes with two or three little urchins giggling in through the doors in front of them, fully distracting me from my duties as sales clerk, to where sometimes I

might have to make up a lie as to why I was suddenly so distracted. And then, I find it impossible to let this woman out of my mind, to tend to my own business in my heart—while she goes about the business of pretending to the public that she has never done this thing in private.

At present, my heart and mind are suddenly distracted from these register duties by the bubble butted blonde teenager walking in the door, whom I suspect already is tainted with this crime, though it could simply be an inherent sluttiness she possesses under her cheerleader exterior. If the girl is not a cheerleader, then I am not a creature of the night. The word of what I am, I absolutely despise, and very nearly cringe at the thought of the truth of how I must live and die.

And the power of this sense is activated and born anew, beyond my lady loving blood alone, when this blonde teenager's 40 year old counterpart walks in behind her. And in my heart and soul, the chimes ring out, even to the vulgar noise of slurping, which is the sound the spirits have laid upon my chest for me to endure, to represent the spit this woman has let fall from her lovely mouth to her daughter's nipples, before she licks and kisses it back up into her mouth again. I know the woman is obsessed with her daughter's breasts, which came in when the girl was fifteen and have not stopped growing since, very likely only halfway to their destination in the future, where Mom will blooble and blobble her way to a wobbling, bobbling ecstasy in them more times than a few, thanking the Almighty in her heart for this gift, of a daughter born and bred to satisfy every secret desire she has that
burns this fire.

This fire, I can see glowing off the woman, flames of cerulean tinted in pitch, where this end of the world thing she does blazes a fervent heat in her daughter's sixteenth year. Yes, I know these things by inherent instinct, as the woman walks through the bookstore with her oversized purse clutched tightly, not content to let the blonde doll do her own thing, and go wandering through the store on her own. She drags her over, ironically, to the self-help section with her, so that she can browse in superiority the titles of the books she knows she'll never need, enjoying the doctors and attractive nobodies and pretty wannabes and worldwide somebodies on the covers, who smile back at her and her daughter in ignorance of what lies beneath. Are there any covers that say *Mother Fuckers: How to Stop Breast Raping Your Daughter?* Probably not. Even the concept would hardly make it onto the shelves in any form, in any guise, as the McKenzie Philips revelation is the safest taboo, the one that people can handle that hardly raises an eyebrow.

But of this thing that I see on this woman, this thing I feel, this thing I smell on her from here, the world is neither prepared for, nor willing to except as a possibility, that from the lower-lower classes and upward, the pervasiveness of this spreads out like the branches

of an oak tree, until I can hardly spend time in the suburban church with a friend who invites me, or time in an expensive restaurant, or especially on a night at the Opera, where I am *not* bombarded with an orgy of truth from one middle aged woman to the next, as my senses are overwhelmed with this secret, Sapphic spirit. It is the last and greatest revelation on human behavior before the endtime, before the world we live in is engulfed in flames, and everything we know and love will be burned to ashes and soot.

Was Daddy on his business trip, when this spirit came unto thee? Where was Daddy, little girl, when Mommy so playfully mentioned how big your breasts (she called them "boobies"), how big your boobies are getting, having held back the complement for several months, after she realized that even as a junior varsity cheerleader, you were already way past double D and growing exponentially, little girl. I can stand it myself no longer, and I have to hand these register duties over to my little slave girl who is overworked and underpaid—the poor little thing works harder than I do and couldn't afford to live on this salary if she worked here full time. I have no pity for Chandra's little light skinned, exploited condition as I descend from my exalted place behind the register counter to go over to where the aura calls me, the aura of mother-daughter perversion, which smells to me like a potent mixture of sweat and perfume.

I slink my sneaky brunette hips over to them as if I am going to speak to them, looking every bit the manager in full blown brunette style, long sleeve forest green turtleneck sweater so uncompromisingly tight over my own bosoms, which are heavier than this blonde thing that calls to me. I walk proudly past the two of them in full literary cloth, deep charcoal gray skirt flailing over my inexplicably brown

boots instead of the black that they should be, smiling in full eye contact with the two of them, cutting the smile away at the last second of eye contact with the nasty woman, who honestly thinks that she hides from me her private obsession with this bubble breasted daughter of hers. A daughter that frankly, I myself should like to compare breasts with naked, as I help her understand what real breast pain and pleasure really are. Yes, I can feel it as completely as the fabric on this winter sweater when I walk past, my Dear, that your body has shaken from the feel of your daughter's breasts in your mouth.

Past the brief little self help section I flow, to where the composer biographies are placed up against the wall shelf. Finding Rossini at first, and then looking for anything on any female composer besides Fanny Mendelssohn, but finding nothing. What exactly it is I am doing over here, I don't know, except that it is like when a cat finds herself wandering around outside a restaurant at the dinner hour, drawn by the distant and forbidden scents wafting through the air toward her from inside. I am privy to the knowledge of thine perversion, Mother Dear, being no stranger to it myself, being that the spirit came to me when I was twelve. Yes, I was twelve, when the spirit came unto me. I was twelve, when the spirit of Woman hath come. I was twelve, when the librarian and kindergarten teacher who was my mother let it out, and taught me that the mind of Eve is passed down through the generations, and that man has no

concept of the fullness of woman, and of what it means to hearken unto the refrain "Woman is Wayward."

As I fake browse these books, Dear Mother, breathing in the scent of you and the daughter I want to eat alive, the daughter whose blood and screams I so desperately want to feed upon, I am aware of what you think was done in secret, when you held this beautiful bubble breasted thing down on the bed and pulled her soft, flopping breasts so high up into your mouth, when you closed your eyes and let the spirit take over your body, when you let it out of your brain and into your blood. I am no stranger to this, Dear Mother Mom, my Dear Mother Lover, being that the woman who gave birth to me had already practiced the pretty little girls hugging her neck and kissing her hard and firm on the lips, which she did so unashamedly in public, choosing at least one of them every year to introduce to the fruit of the forbidden tree, before graduating to the library at Teen Heaven. I know, Dear Woman, what it is between thine daughter and thee, that you believe is so surreptitiously hidden in this bookstore, as you turn to drift to where the *Twilight* saga rests in waiting.

Such a cute little fantasy it is that waits for thine daughter and thee, Dear Mother, while I resist so valiantly the urge to follow you to the other side of the store with more than just my eyes, seeing so clearly the way you felt the energy expand in your body that day, as you held your daughter's breast in your mouth—the way the feeling went through you like the blast wave from ground zero, to make you have to fight to keep your body from shaking more than once, not

even aware of the way your daughter stared at you in amazement of what lust you, Church Lady, are so completely capable of. I see, Dear Woman, how you slide your hand between your daughter's legs in the proper place, the improper place, to make this fifteen year old girl shudder from the connection made, as she watches her beautiful mother pull her big breast into her mouth, and feel the tingle and tickle of tragedy take a towering and traumatic hold of her body.

But this fifteen year old I see with you, Dear Lady, who is sixteen now—this fifteen year old I see with you in her room, she hath excited you to something so far beyond, so far past what you could ever control or resist—causing you to lie down on your back, and have her climb on top of you, and without words, slide her fifteen year old self between your legs, where the underwear cloth must come together in friction, as the cushion between your greatly swollen selves. Lie there, Suburban Queen, with your eyes wide open, to watch this beautiful, heavy breasted young girl writhe herself onto thee, to bring back the energy that only echoed through you a moment before, but which now has threatened to return in tragic intensity, brought forth by the look of deep anguish and defeat on her young face, and the look of her gigantic young breasts swollen and exposed under her shirt before thee.

Oh, my Dear Lady, your daughter is so naïve to pleasure, is she not? You watch her struggle to hold onto what power there is coursing through her pitiful young body, as you look with awestruck

devastation at the beauty of her corruption, at the glory of her downfall as she writhes into thee. You want her so desperately to touch her own breasts, do you not? But you dare not speak a word into this delicate wave of action coalesced, lest you disband it in hopelessness and regret. As your daughter works herself into this rhythm she cannot cease, to try and climb a hill she cannot reach, I see you reach up and grab onto the swollen breast that hangs free, Dear Mother, which sends a shot through your heart into your groin, as she watches your expression crumble to the madness of suffering, as you cry out to the Almighty God, in the sorrow of fear and tragedy.

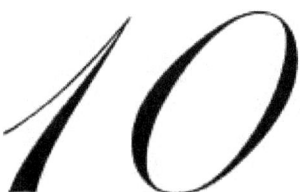

*I* can spot a motheress on the street. I can see it in her eyes. It is a secret that has been building up, gathering steam, gathering strength and momentum, until it threatens to explode. This is the female Mother Lover's Society, the generation of women who have been trained to crave the taste of their own mother's cunt, who have been trained to crave the sound of their own mother's orgasm, who have been trained to crave the feel of their own mother's trembling and loss of sanity in the bedroom, whether on top of this perverted woman, or lying underneath her, delighting while they squeeze the soft Momma Curves, while they watch her get lost

in her missionary mission, to pound herself to the orgasm of her natural life.

These are the Daughters of Perversion. The Daughters of Depravity, who have abandoned the natural use of the man for their ultimate pleasure, who have learned to enjoy the taste of forbidden fruit, whose conscience is seared with a hot iron, that they become immune to the poison of bitter wormwood to the soul. Unlike us, these mother lovers are made and not born, walking the streets in their pitiful, corporate disguises, so many of them in the refuge of churchified hypocrisy, ripe to pass this craving on to any young girl they can get their hands on. To begin this girl on their now predatory path, whose end result is oftentimes a string of victims from six to sixteen, who are indoctrinated into our secret society, where the Mommy Game is private, pervasive, and positively prohibited to speak of.

I am a motheress by trade. Whose interest vacillates between the older and the younger, where sometimes I imagine a sophisticated, sexy older woman on top of me, pinning my arms and biting my neck while I scream, or imagining myself on top of some naïve little bubble butted twit who thinks that the truth lies in the boredom of a boy's cock, where I am in grieving to have my breasts in her mouth, then to smother her with the weight of my own body until I begin to weep from the painful pleasure passing through. Loving so much the corruption of her innocence, the loss of her purity, the devastation of her naïveté, the shock of unfathomable and unwanted pleasure she feels from a woman twenty years older than herself, laid on top of her in a desperation unknown, undiscovered, and unbelieved by the dimwitted masses, who continue to believe that women are

wholesome, and are not the perverse and predatory purveyors of what is a shame to speak of.

And as it stands to reason, I cruise the world in the comfort cushion concept, that *luck has no morality,* and that it rains upon the just and the unjust. As I listen to the bubble breasted, little blonde tweet, twittering something to me about finding some SAT Prep something or another—the same blonde girl that I had seen with her mother in the store a few weeks ago, before the world became buried in a layer of ice and snow—I am content, as I escort her to the academic books, that I am, in her mind, the most beautiful woman she has ever seen. Whether or not this is true is irrelevant, because in the next few minutes of this little motheress' life, I am going to *make* it true, until I know that the look of my eyes is burned into her mind, and the scent of my Paris Perfume is burned into her memory.

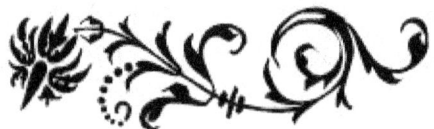

After the requisite smiling is done. When the ridiculous small talk has come and gone. This little motheress is convinced that I am a golden apple at the top of a tree filled with red ones, and she is more than glad while I wait for her to ring up her books which are a waste of money and will be a waste of time. I wonder why, as I watch this pretty young thing in her jeans and white winter coat at the counter, I wonder why it is that every mother so desperately wants her daughter to go to Harvard, Yale, or Princeton. Encouraging them to get in every club and organization, to volunteer for every job and internship and charity—these are the little blue eyed, white toothed

princesses that smile their way through the stench of hospitals and homeless shelters as volunteers, padding these early resumes with their parents' desperation to see them on the go 24 hours a day, 7 days a week until they have climbed the mountain of childhood success. For mothers, this mountain summit is their daughter's acceptance into Harvard, Yale or Princeton, if not the first rate alternatives Dartmouth or Columbia, or even the lesser glories of Wellesley or Vassar, even over the rest of the Ivy League nonsense. I am compelled by something greater than desire, something beyond instinct to connect with this little Patricia, to walk Miss Bubble Butt Bones and Breasts to her mother's big, silver gray Buick, to listen to her go on about how she has no desire to be a doctor or a lawyer, or any other such silliness, and that she would be content to work at Bed, Bath and Beyond and Belk's for the rest of her "miserable life," as she puts it.

"You sound like you need a break from the stress," I say. "Do you have a curfew? Are you allowed to go out at night?"

"I can get away with staying out 'til ten sometimes. It depends on where I am. My grades are good, so I can get away with it."

The cold wind whirls a flurry of snow at the blonde temptress, causing her to wipe a strand of hair from her eyes.

I obey the voice from within, giving place to pure instinct, like a leopard crouched in the lower branches of a tree.

"Well, before we freeze to death," I say, stepping forward to where she is at the driver's side, my black leather boots crunching the thin layer of snow, "I just have one question. Where would you like to have dinner tonight?"

The look on her face. The look in her eyes is the tragedy of human existence.

Which is Fate.

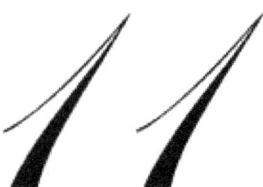

$\mathcal{T}$he snows of our discontent have begun to fall, swirling and drifting their sustained rage above and all around us as we walk. I was more than happy to listen to her pathetic attempt at teenage depth over dinner, caring as much for the rare cooked, bloody delicacy of a New York strip as for the look of her pink and pretty mouth as she rambled on. In our early evening stroll through the big mall parking lot after dinner, I am thankful that the craving I feel in my body does not quite rise to bloodlust, and that perhaps, regardless of what happens to her tonight, she may actually live to tell the tale.

Maybe.

"How come my Mom can't think like you, Jeannie?"

I notice that in the snowy glow of the amaranthine nighttime, the beauty of her young face is as the strawberry crème dessert my body craves.

"I can't even begin to talk like this to my Mom, or my aunts or any of her friends. Even my friends—they're all fucking dead from the neck up about anything else but grades and boyfriends, and *"my Mom took me to this and my Mom took me to that, and Mom bought me this and Mom bought me that.* I wish they would all just shut the *fuck* up about their Moms. Every one of my friends, I swear they all worship their Moms like they're Hilary Clinton or somebody. One of my friend's Mom is the Mayor's second wife for God's sake. One of my friend's Mom is a freaking judge. A *judge*."

"And *your* Mom?"

"I hate to say it, but she's just a rich bitch who thinks she's hot because she's pretty. I wish she could get a good look at you. You look just like Wonder Woman."

"What about your father?"

"Just like everybody else's Dad, he's never home. Always on business trips. I hardly even know him. What about *your* father?"

"I never knew him. Never cared to."

In this snowbound, winter's hesitation, I can feel the rising tide of her next concern, which she has been dying to fully engage me on,

from our second meeting at the book store, to the restaurant, to our stroll through the busy mall, to this snowy walk under the lights, toward the unwelcome sight of her mother's Buick which awaits.

"When did you know?" she says. "How can somebody like you be a lesbian?"

Truthfully, her naïve confusion, colored by the thinly veiled hypocrisy is heartbreaking.

"Now *that,* is a good question," I say, as we leave our lucky stroll behind in early evening white, seeking the warm refuge of Buick pseudo-luxury. She turns the key, rolling us through the nighttime snow, back to where my Sonata sits in repose.

"I've really enjoyed our time together," I say. "I hate curfews myself. Don't you?"

"I told you. As long as I keep straight A's. What can she do? Not a damned thing, that's what."

I am mesmerized by every motion of blonde hair and thin, pearly white fingers fumbling about, clicking buttons and switches until the Morisette Hymn begins to play, and her vaguely erroneous, but well meaning interpretations of the tragic ironies of life. As we ride the snowy streets of this town, I can feel her desperation to explode in the loud mouthed chorus, and the reluctant restraint she must show over top her burning, cheerleader's blood. What feeling of admiration I have had for this young girl begins to swirl into mild contempt, and the scent of her is suddenly as sweet as a stroll past where the pastries are made.

I am glad that I don't know the words to this ancient, endtime anthem, so I don't have to lie through my smile as I refuse to sing.

"It's amazing," she says. "I don't even really know you, Jeannie. Yet I've never been this comfortable with anybody before in my life. I can't explain it but I feel like I can tell you anything."

Oh really, Miss Blonde Snow Bunny! What secret do you have, that runs so deep as the bottom of the Pacific! What endtime revelation is it that lies at the tip of your lying little tongue, held prisoner behind the walls of your pearly white little teeth? What is the source of this second scent I witness, that flows off you in tandem with your own?

"You never did answer my question," she says.

"About why I have a wife instead of a husband?"

"Yeah."

There are portals that open in the fabric of time. Spaces between what is, and what is surely meant to be.

"There's a park a couple miles down Silas Creek. A nice spot— picnic tables. No traffic. I'll bet the snow there is beautiful."

"You mean now? I gotta get home."

And it is here, where what gifts and talents we possess take over. Where our hopeless desperation provides us a vulnerability, a likeability, a power that cannot be resisted or understood.

"I gotta get home too. But I can't."

"How come?"

"Because of you. Because I know I'll never get another chance like this night ever again. Even if it's just another hour, I know I have to spend it talking to you. We'll break curfew together."

And in her silence, I see her warning instinct fade, as she turns to look at a face of sophistication and W.A.S.P. beauty unrivaled. As she turns the car away from lighted suburban safety, toward the blackness of the brief stretch of wooded highway, something inside her is as a voice stifled, that she may not hear what desperation it must speak, nor what devastation of foreboding there is to tell.

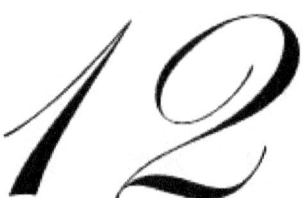

The evening snowfall over Richmond blankets us in the warmth of solitude, parked away from the blaring lights of earthly progression, where only a single, solitary light illuminates the drifting snow, covering the woodland park around us in a field of snowy white.

"I've never shared that with anyone," I say, unable to reel in that most burning part of who I am, as I hear a song from the radio whining something about dragon fire on the mountainside, and the burning forest trees of eschatology.

"I have to go home now," she says, the ivory white of her face giving way to the rosy touch of a rapid heartbeat, and muscles suddenly immobilized in the cold.

"I don't want you to go," I say, locking pale blue eyes with her—sliding next to her in full height and dominance of mind over matter.

"Please," she says. "Let me go."

Already, I hear the breathlessness in her naïve young voice, and I am fascinated by the well of tears that threaten to flow. If she blinks once, I know the tears will flow.

Does she blink?

She does.

And I lose my ability to breathe for a fraction of a second, as I quickly, athletically, straddle her in the back seat, while this dragon fire song plays softly in the air around us. In my long skirt and boots, I remove my coat whilst I press down on her, relishing the noisy sound it makes. I am reminded underneath the coat, that it is not possible for my sweater to feign the appearance of flatness against my body.

"What are you doing?" she says. "I'm not a lesbian."

"You're not being fair," I say, my voice having deepened to a place far and away below. "I told you a secret. About what Betty Greenwood did to me."

"Who's Betty Greenwood?"

"You tell me. My name is Jeannie Greenwood."

"Betty Greenwood was your mother?"

In silence, I stare.

Mercilessly.

"Tell me your secret," I say. "While you roll my sweater up above my breasts."

"I don't have a secret," she says. "I swear."

"Roll up my sweater," I say. Pressing upon her the full weight of command, that she may not resist, as though programmed and predestined to comply. Even while her hands fumble at the bottom of my sweater, the merest touch of her fingers against my body twitches me from my stomach to my groin, and I must readjust my hold and pressing tight against her. In silence, in unspoken depth of command, I watch her roll up my sweater, to reveal the biggest bra she has ever imagined, and never imagined that she would ever see in this lifetime.

"Pull my bra up," I say. "Until both my breasts are hanging out."

This, she does. As I shudder from the light scraping of fabric against my nipples, as the two enormous worlds of flesh collide with this world of space around them.

"Oh, my God I've never seen…that's *impossible.*"

I can assure you, my Dear.

It's possible.

"Put your mouth on my nipple," I say, in such a deep, breathy tone, "while you think of the first time you fucked your mother."

"But I didn't…"

My hands go immediately to her mouth, in a strength that I know she cannot process, as though she is suddenly in the grip of a band of padded iron.

I take my hand away, and watch her without mercy as she fumbles to give suck, causing my entire body to flinch from the flick of her tongue, and the suckling touch of her cold, wet lips to them. I take this breast up into my own hand, raising it up that she may give suck, looking away from her in rapt amazement, of what pleasure

this is to every inch of my body, feeling as though I may drift away from her as a spirit, and float away as a phantom in the snow.

"Like you *mean* it," I say, "like you're sucking it for milk."

And I feel her sucking transform from a vacuum suck to a vacuum suckle, every pull of which across the waving of her tongue rises me higher up, until I have a sense of near levitation, and the feeling that every drop of water in my groin may gush forth in ruptured fashion. I take my breast from her mouth, lest I lose my sanity, and I lock my lips to hers, grunting full and deeply into her mouth, not caring at all what pleasure or pain these rumblings must send into her body.

I release her tongue in the fullness of a kissing, suckling pull, aware now of the look of terror in her eyes, a look that I have seen before.

"When did you fuck your mother," I say.

"But I swear I didn't. I *swear.*"

In a calmness, a peace that lulls her into false tranquility, I take both her hands into mine, my exposed breasts pressed so gigantic against her white sweater fabric, and I squeeze her fingers together on both her hands like two vices, to hear the music of her screaming echo into the night.

"Tell me."

"I can't... I don't remem— "

The melody of her scream echoes deep and loudly into my body again, until I cannot resist the pre-tremble that must be, which lightly spasms my spirit from head to toe.

"I was fifteen," she says. "She made me raise up my cheerleader sweater," she says.

"You're lying, bitch. I can *feel* you lying."

And the rondeau, the third melody of screams bursts forth from her, with her shaking her head in madness, until she cannot resist the pain of fingers nearly broken, nor keep the barrier of hypocrisy raised against the truth inside.

"It was in the bathroom! I swear to God it was in the bathroom!"

And my body settles in for the ride of this truth chariot, and images of mother daughter perversion, and suburban secrets and depravities revealed.

"Last summer," she says, face burdened with tears and terror. "In the hotel on a cheerleader trip. She was on the toilet naked. Then she made me sit on her and bounce up and down on her real hard. I wasn't really sure she was serious until I opened my eyes and saw the look on her face. She was staring at my breasts and she started saying *oh my God* over and over again, and while I was bouncing up and down on her a big, loud scream just came out of her. I swear to God, it scared me to death it was so loud, it was like a siren..."

And amidst the siren of her mother's voice, is mixed the sound of my own, as this girl is witness to the whiteness of my eyes rolled back, and the strength of force in the trumpet blaring of my voice, and the end-of-the-world trembling in every muscle in my body. In the haze of a slow motion dream, the reality of our little world fades

from my vision, until I am shown the whiteness of her neck in singular place of purpose, and I am pushed down to it by the unseen hand of pure instinct, until I can feel the warmth of sweetness flowing down my throat like wine, and the screaming of her last breath exploding into the nighttime winter air around me.

*Jonathan Lovejoy*

# Iris Greenwood Rides the Wind

# 13

*I*ris Greenwood rides the Wind. Each step upon the
unforgiving breeze of icy November air, that seeks to drown her
in the passing of Indian Summer's memory. So elegant and
beautiful, this flower among weeds, she is, stepping the heights of
Brunette Beauty. Away from the seventh and eighth grade halls of
learning, through the rainy mists to her chariot in waiting. Leader of
young minds, shaper of future destinies, this brunette lovely, rain
cloak flowing in league with her skirt, to ride her elegantly in the
breeze. Teacher of the Year, reigning over these little seventh and
eighth grade souls. The envy of every other. Envy swirled into
desperation for some. But knowing already, somehow, that the
Widow Greenwood is not theirs to possess. A woman impossible to

look upon. Whose power is impossible to pull away from. Who has the love and respect of this little eastern Virginia town.

Somewhere just south and east of Richmond. Teacher today by the rains of Melancholy Bay, the cold rains of Autumn Gray, blown in from the shores of the raging waters of the Atlantic, and what offshore storms are held at bay.

Iris Greenwood rides the Wind. Adrift from the last touch of the school concrete, into the plush safety of her rolling chariot. Barely able to touch the keys to the ignition. Feeling the tremble start in her heart, then flow outward past the arms to the extremities. Jangling the keys like a chime in the winds of an approaching storm. Through effort, managing to pass the key through, into the ignition, as her hand receives the fullness of the tremble, on the eve of her 40th victim. A serial killer among women, a bone collector of souls, abductor of the innocence of young girls and women. Unable to start the car in this cold, autumn rain, as she thinks of the taste of Carmen Carolini. The feel of the girl's lips and tongue. The powder taste of her ripe young breast in her mouth.

Remembering the way that her own body made the decision for her, when young Carmen Carolini walked into her classroom, the new transfer from below the southern border, the fourteen year old shapely from down below. *Carolina Carolini,* the spirits whispered to her, when the hippy, breasty young thing sat in dead-eyed demurity. *Number 40,* was the spirit torment in her eyes, when the

Carolini girl sat down. Knowing already that this child would not see the halls of her ninth grade year. That the horizon of her fifteenth year would never come. Knowing already that the fates have willed this—this new girl, in the hour before her lunch period, when there are no teachers for her to report to within the hour.

Iris Greenwood rides the wind. Eyes closed in a brief commitment of recall. To remember the flash of future revelation her body gave her when the tall, brown skinned guidance counselor brought her in. As she finds her seat—knowing already what form the young girl's death will take. Hardly able to concentrate on the rambling, rolling rigmarole of English Grammar and Composition, as her mind feeds her the image of the girl naked underneath her, her arms pinned, her legs spread wide open, while Iris grinds herself groin to groin, smothering her naïve young body with breasts played on the key of G Major, above the tiny, fleshy waist curve, widened hips squeezed and released in impending agony.

Iris Greenwood rides the Wind. Cranking the car in the rain. In the pain of her body's recollection, and the rising torment of *Number 40* in her ear. Unable to put the car in gear, as she feels the softness of the girl's overdeveloped young breast in her mouth in the locked classroom, where the shade is pulled down over the frosted glass, and the lights are killed for every intent and purpose. Iris can hardly breathe a steady breath anymore, as she remembers the shot that went through her body, as she pressed a kiss to the young Italian girl's virgin mouth. Holding the back of the girl's head as she presses the deep kiss—letting the kiss do its bidding upon her flesh, so that there is no dignity left to salvage, when her body spasms in the daytime dark of her locked classroom. Letting a single grunt vibrate

into the young girl's hopeless, condemned young body. Feeling it tremble onto the girl's tongue pulled inside. Knowing that the dampness at her eyes are the tears of instinct. The impossibility of backwoods conquest achieve in the civilized, open air. To have conducted this symphony of depravity to perfection.

The new girl. Her favorite student with the musical name. The musical young breasts in D minor. The musical young hips spread and bubbled. In this toil and trouble she burns, having called and chosen another, not just to bounce into corruption, but to soon choke and smother, then feed upon the slowly pumping sweetness that ebbs and flows underneath the milky white skin. Then to draw every drop for safekeeping. Then dispose of what cold and lifeless flesh doth still remain.

Iris Greenwood rides the Wind. Smiling a laugh of victory, of disbelief to herself. Cruising the rains of this Virginia Autumn. Remembering the look, the feel, the scent, the taste, of Carmen Carolini.

Iris Greenwood rides the Wind. The wind of eschatology.

# Footprints in the Snow

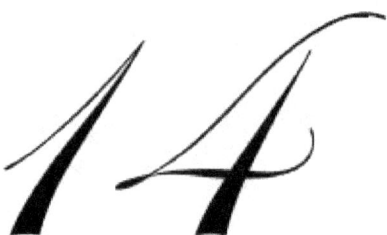

$\mathcal{I}$ will not deny my allegiance to the cold. To the snows that fall on a lonely winter's night. I am more at home among the flurries and the ghosts that fly, than sitting in some warm book store café or restaurant among the middle class mindlessness, the droning of *me*-ishness and manufactured civility. Smiles that hide hearts of evil that I can feel, teeth blared as the crocodile, in waiting to tear the flesh from one another's bones in instinct and fear.

I crunch the miles through the nighttime snow, along the isolated streets of this town, so far removed in my heart from the blonde bitch I just unburdened from the pain of this life. Wanting so desperately to have been able to take my time somewhere in the nude, and drain

the rest of her white body of the four quarts that are left, that will soon be drained anyway when her body is found. Oh, how my tiny little footprints would intrigue in the light of day, as they disappear into the icy confusion of the highway and beyond!

I walk slowly along in the drifting snow, glad for what sudden and dramatic sea of flurries now swirl, as if in response to my thoughts on the trivialities of man's will, to ensure that by morning, the entire city will be entombed in a sea of white, with only dreams and memories of footprints in the snow.

The city lights bathe the last of my snowy walk with her blonde memory. Attacking me with images of her beautiful young face in the throes of fear and naivete, in a futile, if not feeble attack at my sensibilities. A part of me wishes to release a laugh of complacency, a smile or a snicker of mocking control, held in check by the common sense of what I know, which is that mankind is to not be deceived, for God is not mocked. And I know that somehow, it is an answer to a dark calling I have been bestowed with from birth, that gives me the profound lust and ability I possess, that no ordinary man or woman could ever dominate or control me one on one, except for one that so often haunts my dreams and nightmares. It is the one who lives somewhere in the Virginia countryside, the librarian turned recluse, who is now comfortable lurking and drifting alone. Though I try not to let it be so, I hear the voice of Mother call to my spirit, even to my blood so often in the night, to where I am aware of its ghostly pull from somewhere along the horizon of my road, just

past every dawn on my journey through time. As to exactly how and when, I do not know. But everything that I am knows that I must someday leave behind these amaranthine lights, and go to where the starlight is unburdened by the artificial glow of mankind's futility.

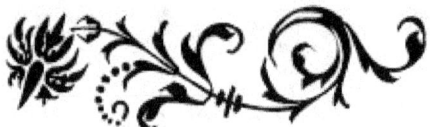

As my spirit brings the whispers of another Iris, one that echoes from the days of my youth, I am chilled inside by the pulling of these two women, the drawing of my attention from my present time, and my desire to be warmed again in the arms of the woman I love. I brave this new and icy chill from the ages, endeavoring to push their beauty aside for the moment, but how? Knowing that it is the old time call of the wild that has suddenly began to torment me, here, anew at the age of 33, when I know that for the rest of my life, I am going to fuck and kill women.

And this desire has grown, to show itself to me tonight in the snow, leaving the template, the beginning of my future, lying cold and alone in the abandoned car. She will be found tomorrow, I know—it is the newest project that I add to the one my Anya and I had already begun. And I am burdened by two spirits passed down, from the mind of the other Iris down to my mother Elizabeth, or Betty as the world once knew, that my primary lust is the sweat and blood of young girls in full blown, sexual naivete, while part of me wishes to be dominated into screams by a mother.

These two spirits are passed down, making me sick and twisted among women, that I know my next young victim must feel the

pressure of my girl cock when she dies, and before too long I am going to have to feel the weight of my own mother pressed down upon it in weeping.

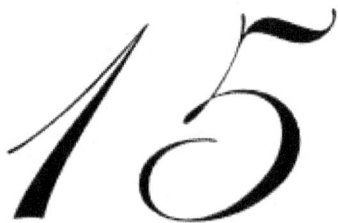

The drive down these pristine, suburban streets never ceases to amaze me. Five hundred thousand dollars worth of tranquility bought and paid for, so that savings and investment accounts guarantee the presence of loan money and high line credit scores, so that cash and capital gain are never far from the equation of this life. Even while I am lulled to this late evening tranquility by the soft glow of lights from every distance, illuminating the grand, brick homes in the fields of snow, this weather carries my mind up and away, to the briefest glimpse of the Anya bloodline, whose mother and grandmother killed her father when she was five, an act that she witnessed and processed as the origins of her misandry, her youth

images of her own father being dominated into screaming by her mother and grandmother, who was laid heavy and strong on top of him while her mother held him strong from underneath. Anya saw only his dying, kicking feet, and heard his pathetic, choking scream, as her strong, heavy hipped grandmother growled and shook her head like a wild animal at the naked man's poor neck until he neither moved nor made another sound. What Anya saw next fertilized the seed planted, as the man was taken off the bed by both naked women and unceremoniously covered, as they returned to the bed and wrestled each other for dominance, until Anya's grandmother was laid in full on top of Anya's mother, her Russian grandmother then slamming herself in strong, regular rhythm to her daughter until she executed something akin to a wolf howl.

Female domination, hearkened from the cold, night woods of a Russian landscape—brought to the icy wilderness of Minnesota's unforgiving winters, where her mother and grandmother still live to this day. Having killed and fed unrepentedly on the blood of women and girls, having no taste for the "salt and stench of a man's blood." Spending many hours and days in exploration of north woods country, not shy to discover what camping grounds and open, wooded park areas where the foolish are fit to frequent—always so delighted when one of their buried victims would show up missing on the news. The woods behind their house is a cold, lonely graveyard of secrets, and victims that number a quantity too high to be believed.

*"You're not like me,"* Anya would often say, *"you're so sweet—so filled with mercy for them."* Oh, Dear Anya, as the vast and picturesque beauty of our home approaches me tonight, oh, my dearest Anya Shier, born from the Enya and Veronica Lenardovsky line—a line of wild, animalistic creatures of no remorse, who take what they need from womankind without conscience, and without reservation or regret. Bitter, blue collar beasts, they are. Terrors of the night woods, the scourge of humanity's twilight in history. Of what need should my Love have to visit them ever again, lest she risk being added to their collection of bones in the latter day woods of the North.

I am afraid, dear Anya.

As I roll this suburban chariot past the golf course lawn covered in winter white, as our southern mini-mansion extends warm greetings to me in the night, I am burdened by fear from what things I must speak, and of what things I imagine that your hot, Russian ancestry may inspire your heart, your mind, and your body to bring down upon me without mercy.

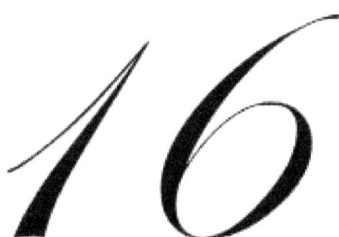

*T*he trappings of upper class suburban life greet me with open arms when I open the door. I am not jaded to the tall, glowing white walls, and the space that extends to a remarkable distance across the huge livingroom to the carpeted staircase. I take the fearful steps past the gigantic portrait of Creation in nude form, the truth of silken white breasts and hips in *Biblis,* stepping past Bouguereau's unnamed beauty in repose toward the staircase in waiting, waiting to light my first step into action, phasing me into a brief trip across this part of the timeline, to the most uncertain part of my future impending, that I have felt in such a long time. Each step I take is more nerve racking, more fearful than the last, as if I am climbing

the rocky incline of a mountain pass, toward the darkened cave of some prehistoric creature that awaits. But I take a deep breath and shake my head, as if to shake myself awake from the onset of an unwelcomed dream, telling myself that it is not a blood thirsty monster that awaits. It is only my Anya. Whom I know loves me with a fever, with such an intense loyalty as to be possessive, to where sometimes I have to resist the urge to manipulate her obsession.

I take the last steps along this journey through time, landing at the top of the staircase a second, a millennium from where I once was, walking the hall of portraits to where the next part of my journey awaits, through the open door of the upper room.

Sheltered from the nighttime snowfall, Beauty rests in the sleep of the ages. I am suddenly no longer ill at ease, as I begin to remove my long, black winter coat on the way to the big closet. Part of me hopes that she will soon stir away from whatever tantalizes or torments her night vision, to come back from the other world into this one, and keep me from feeling so lost and alone. But the other part of me is glad that she is dead to the world, that she might remember these

little lights and sounds as part of her nighttime repose, as part of whatever dreamscape she may be lost in.

In the closet, I make slow and steady work of each part of my civilized self, the calf high black boots, the button down cashmere of the deepest pewter, the matching turtleneck underneath, that grieves to carry the burden of my bosom in perpetual immodesty, that was so perfectly hidden by the sweater that now hangs in the room sized closet with the rest. I unzip the long, charcoal skirt, still amazed at the size of what I see in the full length mirror, bound up inside the big, black lace fabric. The pale, extreme voluptuousness is arresting, to be sure, curves in stark contrast to the black cloth pieces that highlight rather than hide the truth.

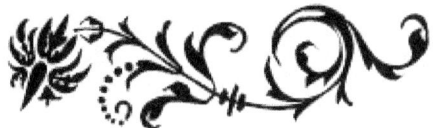

I slide the thigh high stockings down and away, glimpsing the woman in the mirror who does likewise, unable to pretend not to notice the curse of the macromastic bosom. It is a cleavage that goes on to infinity from the bra fabric upward, to where most have never seen or imagined could ever really exist in 3D space. It is a physique in hourglass form, made both fit and voluptuous by birth and Predestiny alone. Often causing me to have pity for those who spend so many thousands of dollars to have their natural breasts butchered that they may look like these things I see and carry. Or those women who liposuck and starve and strain themselves in futility, to have this

deeply curved middle that I take for granted, or those women who have conceded that they are slope-backed, meaning hips that are flat from their backs down to their thighs, who have convinced themselves that having a scarecrow butt is desirable. Even so, this naturally curved body I carry is at times more of a curse than a blessing, bringing so much unwanted attention when I wear the wrong clothes, when what lies beneath is too truthfully revealed.

The drawings of the superhero women are not as much of an exaggeration as people may think—as some women do possess such unfathomable curves and body parts to display. I turn to the side, to marvel at what a 36 J cup bra holds in place, and a pair of buttocks born from the Land of Lopez, and the Kingdom of Kardashia. Is it a body that would have me worshipped or ridiculed on the beach? This, I choose not to know. What would the husbands do under their sunglasses when I walked by? What would the wives do under theirs? A sunny time in the surf is not a luxury for me, I fear, being that for reasons unknown, I despise spending too many long minutes in direct sunlight, nor am I particularly attracted to the beauties of a bright and sunny day in the shade.

I finally step into the dark of the bedroom, fully dressed in my two pieces of underwear cloth, to quietly spend time in the porcelain palace, in front of another mirror, when I'm done with whatever else needs to be.

"You *know* you can't sneak past me."

The voice freezes me in midstep, like an icy hand, ghostly and strong, grabbing me by the throat.

"I heard you come in," she says. "It's like I was watching you in my sleep but I couldn't wake up."

"Sorry about that. I should've been quieter."

Bathroom forgotten, I step timidly over to the bed, sitting down nearby her covered legs and feet.

"Jesus *Christ,"* she says, staring at my body. Bewilderedly. "How is that even possible?"

Oh, I can assure you my dear.

It's possible.

"Are you okay, sweetie?"

I lower my head, staring at the white thighs, widened by the sitting.

"Sweetie, you know how I feel about your body," she says, sliding a sleepy hand down my thigh to my knee.

"I think I'm going to quit."

"Quit what?"

"That damned job. I'm sick of it."

"What's really the matter? You worried about that Bridgeman bitch we buried? Nobody's gonna find her here. We parked her car in her own neighborhood for God's sake."

The spirits of remorse drift in again at me from the cold, to touch my eyes to a watery haze.

"I fed tonight."

My voice is low. Almost whispery.

"You *what?"*

I can only sniff back the tears that threaten to flow. Unable to speak. Unable to look her in the eye.

Suddenly, I feel her hand wrapped tightly in my hair, and the burning agony of the pulling upon my scalp. The face I see when I look up at her is the beauty of feminine rage, in the flaxen haired, blue eyed form of an angel of death. As I accept what divine penalty I must finally suffer, I feel the watery edge of my regret finally break, running down the side of my face in full. And perhaps it is the sight of this tear which saves my life, causing her burning look to soften, and the icy stare in her eyes to subside.

I know better than to say a word, as she releases her grip on my hair, and slides a body muscled in feminine, athletic tone in topless splendor off the bed, going into the bathroom and closing the door with remarkable restraint. But the next instant of my life is filled with the sound of a loud *crash* in otherworldly loudness, which is the noise I would imagine would be heard, if crashing vanity mirrors could scream.

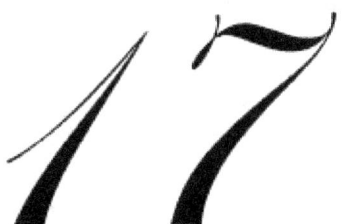

*I*n the gloomy aftermath of the temper that was Hurricane Anya, I rest in uneasy tranquility on the plush, beige sectional, having drifted to sleep with *Biblis* beauty in my vision, half expecting to have endured a nightmare of walking through that mysterious, leafy clearing she is in, and getting attacked and devoured by Anya. But my sleep was plagued only by the intermittent awakenings, and the feeling that she would soon make her way toward me from the top of the stairs. But I made it through this cold and snowy night, further down the timeline still, from my moment on the edge of the bed after that end of the world shattering of glass from the bathroom. I had been immobilized by both fear and

regret, sitting in my underwear on the edge of the bed, bent over with both hands covering my face, until something inside me literally spoke the words *get out of this room.* I can remember not bothering to go the closet for a nightgown, but turning the bed corner in a quiet rush, until I was at the linen closet for an old comforter and a pillow.

The morning slides me awake in the early daytime dark, which tells me that it is time for me to get up anyway, if for no other reason, to deliver that ridiculous bookstore my two weeks notice. I have been blessed with life's lottery, born into a situation that allows me to relinquish my cares about money, and the trapping of empty corporate success. If Anya wants it, she can have it. Strangely enough, there will soon be a corporate position made officially open, when the world is done wondering where Barbara Bridgeman is, and why she's never coming back.

As to my time alone on this huge sofa, sometimes, love and desperation can overcome fear. And when I hear the stirrings of light from upstairs, as I see the waves of sound quiver at the top of the stairs, I know that my time alone in this house is passed for now, even if I must endure what is left of the pain she still has to give.

I am un-chilled by the cold air around me as I walk, still in the huge black bra and tiny underwear, leaving the blanket to mark the place where my nighttime fear and loneliness was laid. I look into the guest bedroom where I see the sound of motion, hearing the shower in the guest bathroom. This is but the tiniest wilderness of hope for me to cross, going through the smaller bedroom to the guest bathroom, so thankful that the door is ajar. If she screams at me, if she threatens this vanity mirror too with my head, I will take it like a woman, and I will bleed willingly my last drop of strength at her feet.

I go into the steamy bathroom, quickly sliding out of the gigantic bra, feeling the great things swing like bells when I bend over, sliding the cloth smoothly and quietly away. There is no glimpse in the mirror image steam, focused only on what steps there are to be taken, and how I might gather myself ready to be beaten in the nude. But when I open the shower curtain, I see only the image of blonde, blue eyed sorrow, a beauty deepened by pain and humility, and she takes my hand immediately, as I step over the sides of the intimate little bathtub. She hugs me in tight, loving desperation, unable to raise her head from beside mine and look me in the eye, forcing me to feel the trembling of repentance in her body, and with the sound of her tearful pleading for forgiveness, swirling in the small, tightly closed shower space around me.

Jonathan Lovejoy

# The Rape

# of Iris

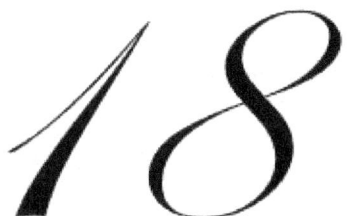

ℰxtreme erotic sensitivity is my curse, if there is such a thing, so that I must endure multiple orgasms when she touches me. From behind me on our bed, she begins to squeeze and work the flesh of my big breasts like she means it, as an early warning signal of what devastations, what pleadings, what weepings there are to come. On our knees, with her pressed tight against me from behind, the pleading has already begun, when she takes both nipples in hand, not for the pleasure of a painful pulling or twisting, but for the pinching and tweaking of my soul's agony, every pinch already warning my body that if this hammering should continue, then what stability there is of me will begin to crumble. It is the curse of

orgasmic insanity, where I can feel myself gripped from the inside and carried aloft, to a place where pleasure knows no bounds, and drifts the unfortunate chosen into suffering. I understand as much as any who have ever been born, there is a God, and the wonders of his creation are beyond the reasoning of man.

Truthfully, I would prefer to be the outlet for her perversion, to endure physical pain for her pleasure, or to be the cushion for her own rise and fall to oblivion. But I know that I am going to have to be severely punished, and for me it begins when she starts to rapidly tweak both my nipples, until my entire body rings the chime of warning, to make me shake my head 'no' while I moan, then to echo this sentiment with the word itself. Knowing what I know of this blast wave inside me, it is a place I do not necessarily wish to be, even voicing the words in futility *"please don't make me cum."* Oh, but what feeble begging for mercy this is, accursed woman! For I am held prisoner by sadism in blonde and blue eyed beauty, and the strength hearkened from the shores of Olympus, along the forests and fields of our most Themyscaran dreams of grandeur.

*"Oh, please have mercy,"* I say in the tragedy of futility again, as I approach the line of no return, wishing so desperately for her to lay me down, to turn me over and relieve my suffering with slappings, bitings and chokings. But this play upon my nipples carries me past the highest heights of where hope is lost, so that I can only hold on to her tightly, pushing back against her in such a pathetic writhing and

loud whimpering, until I am gripped in full by the spirits that carry me aloft, and they dive over the side of this mountain with me straight down, where I am only the rising of one loud, long wailing, that rises to the level of a siren, where after a breath is taken, rises then to the level of a scream. The energy does not course through my body as much as it *becomes* my body, where Anya's touch, her presence is replaced by the sorrow of the ages, and the sufferings of wayward womankind. I can only hold on and scream, a loud and deep woman's scream while she pinches my nipples without ceasing, as the waves crash down upon me like the leading edge of a hurricane come to shore.

As she continues to tweak and pinch my nipples without mercy, I am aware enough of myself to be able to shake my head so rapidly back and forth, pushed back against her while she looks at me without mercy, enjoying the rapid, electric convulsing of my entire being, and the spasmodic shaking of my body from head to toe.

She mercifully releases them so that she can watch the aftermath, so she can feel what energy of Eve hath turned me into, touching a nipple just enough once more, to watch me flinch once mightily, and shake my head "no" in pleading once again.

*"I'm going to have to fuck you,"* she speaks in my ear. So calmly, with such deep and breathy assurance, that I am as a slave in chains,

with naught but the will to be pulled along, until my purpose and destination have been wrought. She gently, firmly pushes me down to all fours, and I am immediately aware of the pressure that touches me from behind, as the *first* of eight minus seven is pushed into the back of me, which calls the spirit back to my hopeless body again, where she grabs me upon the *second* inch slid in, to make me have to moan the cause of my bravery, to carry me across the battlefield of arousal in full, that I may do battle with the next beast which must devour my flesh, until it makes me tremble and scream once again. I perceive the *third* inch slid up into me, which makes me grip the sheets and lower my head, only shaking my head in the pre-cry, in the soft whimpering before the fact, as I feel the *fourth* inch slide past the barrier of reason, to make me understand that this is the Rape of Iris, the Rape of the Sabine Women, and I know that what sufferings have begun in me are destined to continue.

This, I feel in the *fifth* inch and beyond, as the *sixth* and *seventh* slide sublimely into me, until I can already endure not another. But she grips me tighter, as does the spirit that caries me for a ride, and I feel the onset of the thrashing, stormy *eighth,* which crashes against me in merciless warning of what is to come. And then I feel a single, mighty lurch forward, where the *ninth* and final inch blazes forward to the limits of its calling, causing me to exclaim once in this chorus of suffering, this chorale symphony, where the voices in me are indeed an ode to the joys of erotic agony. I feel every inch of herself

strapped on, the fullest expression of her inner woman attached and grown, sliding almost all the way out of me, then slamming back up into me in one hard thrust, to make me lower my head and cry out, a cry for mercy without words, amidst the single, powerful twitching of my body from the trauma.

And I feel the pounding begin, the mighty sliding in and out, accompanied by the bouncing and slapping of flesh, and the loudness of my pathetic whimpering. In this, I can feel the gathering of her energy, and the quiet, angry calling of the word *"bitch,"* accompanied by a renewed vigor in her slamming full against me, until I know that I am soon to be as a lit firework on the fourth of July. This, she seeks to achieve without mercy, repositioning herself, raising up, grabbing me firmly by the waist and going into me like a factory machine, whose purpose is to ream the corruption from some tubular thing or another.

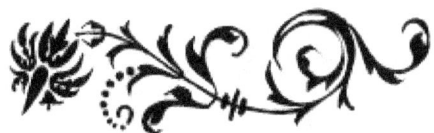

From the strength of this, from the angry energy of it, I know that I am being punished a second time, unable to feign enjoyment, but only to grip the sheets in the fearful whimpering, and breathless pleading of one who has already been devastated once, and is truly afraid to have to endure it again. But already, the fuse has been lit, and every second of this relentless pounding drives the sparkling, hissing fire closer to its destination. But watching me suffer has

finally done its work on her own body, and she must abandon the goal of watching me explode first, and I feel her laid down heavy upon me from behind, grabbing my giant breasts with both hands, gripping her teeth to my ear, slamming into me now a rabbit rhythm of her own desperation, until I hear the warriors screech start inside her, causing her to release my ear in the Cry of the Warrior Queen, as the fuse lights me up without mercy, to send me to the stratospheric heights of another rise and fall.

In the middle of her loud, angry yelling, there is a soprano scream of pure agony, quick and powerful, sharper than a two edged sword, cutting through the both of us with a fiery blade, as I begin to tremble again slightly, as the far end of her battle cry fades to vanishing. Our mouths immediately find their brief connection, which can only be called kissing and licking, with the gruffness of her voice vibrating deeply into me upon my tongue.

Oh, but what tragedies are there left to be! What sufferings, Dear Anya, are left for us to endure!

Lay me down, turn me over, my love! Lay roughly down upon me to rest, before this violent and stormy finale must begin.

She proceeds to open my legs, sliding the member all the way into me, telling me firmly to open my legs, and I know to hold them back as far as I can, so that I cannot anchor myself for this last rise and fall. She takes the gigantic breasts in hand, pushing them together up underneath her, that they may cushion her last ride,

looking me in the eyes as she pins both my arms back underneath me. Already, I know that the pressure of her laid upon my breasts, the clamping of my arms, and the relentless missionary pounding into me are going to make me have to call upon the name of God, in prayer that I may not suffer his wrath in the final hour of this judgment. But when her pounding begins, it is as the moving forward of a train at the onset, where no force in nature can stop it, and I am compelled to a genuine plea for mercy, asking her to please have mercy, but knowing that I could not break the grip I am in if I tried, and neither could she from the grip of this sadism and song.

Her body sings the Rhythm of the Amazons, as her groin begins the unmerciful up and down, causing me to hold my head back in the pre-cry, the weeping moan that has already begun, knowing that somehow, this will devastate my body and soul to ruin, and have me ponder the curse of the very day I was born. And I am assured of this, when the unwanted pleasure beckons, and the spirit looks upon me with unforgiving eye, grabbing me, carrying me upward, higher and higher up again, while I am held at the near edge of a weeping that threatens, that is drawn far out in a quiet, moaning plea for God's mercy.

But Anya's focus is gathered this time, so that the thirst of her own body is quenched, so that now her angry soul must be fed,

allowing her the strength and concentration to pound into me at will, a potent mix of fast and slow rhythms, slower, faster, thunder, and then lightning, until she is bound and determined to see my sanity crumble, to see me die a violent death in spirit, to see me humbled again to a place of knowing that there is nowhere on earth that I could run, nowhere in the universe I could hide, where she could not find me, and make me call out to Heaven for mercy.

And this heavenly spirit of uncompromising power looks at me without mercy again, and I shake my head in denial once more, as the perfect rhythm between fast and slow begins my descent into madness, as I am flown, dived from the top of the world toward the bottom, beginning the wail, but stopping it to take a breath, then wailing my hopelessness through the walls of our bedroom, across the field of snow, calling for the mercies of Almighty God and Christ the Lord.

# Iris Greenwood

# Chimes the Night

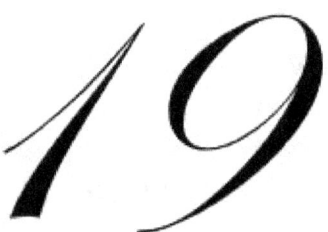

*I*ris Greenwood chimes the night. To prime victim no. 40, for her last and otherworldly flight. Having already whirled all of the other neighborhood girls and schoolgirls home. The ones who were called. The chosen few. The eighth grade little pretties invited to study at Ms. Greenwood's house in the afternoon. Teacher of the Year. Mother of one, so they think. A little 12 year old beauty named Jeannie. Little Jeannie Greenwood, and her *grandmother* Iris. Teacher of the Year.

A prestige gathering, it is. The gathering, chirping and chattering of little pubescent pretties. Smiling, laughing, eating, drinking, not

pretending to be merry. It is young girl paradise at Ms. Greenwood's house. In the big, pretty brick house at Breezewood Park Estates. The house on the hill. The category four hurricane of a house. Whirling a wind of privilege. A scent too irresistible for them. A neighborhood too magnificent to ignore. The teacher who lives in the place with the golf course lawns. The Greenwood Estate. Mothers in a line to get their girls to Ms. Greenwood's house. Teacher of the year.

This is a November Saturday come and gone. When the little girls have spent the whole day at Ms. Greenwood's. First, to the museum. Then, to the mall. Then, to the McDonald's. Such a collection of clattering little cuties. Pre-cheerleaders. Pre-scholars. Little pre-workaholic wannabees. All of them witches in waiting.

Except one.

This one, Ms. Greenwood, rides in the car with your little girl. Your little granddaughter they all think is your daughter. Little Iris Jean. Little Jeannie.

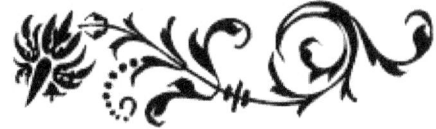

Fourteen year old Carmen Carolini, having won the grand prize. The sleep over. The special time at Ms. Greenwood's house, through the weekend until Sunday afternoon. Parents burdened by the thrill of it. The wealthy beauty, with the Master of Arts in English Literature. Gathering the select few under her wing. Preparing them

for high school. Putting them on track to the promised land. To the place where the Ivy dreams come and go. The place where she hearkens from. To the Greenwood halls of Princeton, they aspire.

She does not have to try. Those eyes. Those cheeks. Those lips. Careful not to hide the figure that they pretend not to notice. A woman they are glad to flaunt in front of their pathetic husbands. To mock them with what they cannot have. To bask in the glory of her arrival in their lives. In their daughter's lives.

Dr. and Mrs. Carolini. New in the south. So glad to have their daughter embraced by the beautiful teacher. Teacher of the Year.

They roll the lights of earthly progression. The manmade lights of the evening day. In the glow of the deep twilight, nearby the edge of night. The teacher, her daughter, and the daughter Carolini. Ready to settle down in the upperclass brick estate. To get into their night clothes, to popcorn a snack, to watch a movie on the big TV screen. To spend another weekend learning the Greenwood way of life. Both mother and 'daughter.'

The car cruises the asphalt path to luxury. Nearby the perfectly greened and manicured lawn of privilege. In the driveway of duplicity, she sends little Jeannie to the front of the house—to unlock the door and go up to her room.

*"I have to talk to Carmen about school,"* she says. *"I'll be up in a minute."* As to what feeling little Jeannie Greenwood perceives from her grandmother in the twilight, this, she does not know. Only that

there are energies that flow through time, and perceptions of them that come and go. Little Jeannie gathers her grandmother's keys, bewilderedly, in lovely little lips tucked in, and hurries obediently across the front of the grand and softly lit brick home, clumsily opening the front door.

In the car, as if triggered by the closing of the door—a slam so loud in hearing heightened to perceive—the beautiful woman leans over to the fourteen year old girl, placing her mouth upon the girl's lips, opening it into a deep, sucking kiss, pulling away, staring at the young girl's confusion without mercy, and without remorse.

*"You're the most beautiful little girl I've ever seen,"* the woman says. *"You want to stay with me tonight, don't you?"*

But what can she do, my Iris Dove, but tuck her maturing little lips in like fashion as your granddaughter, and nod her head "yes" while she stares at you, unable to move? Unable to blink?

*"Kiss me,"* the woman says. Eyes wide open. Watching her little slave push her face into hers. Feeling her resistance in the kiss.

Loving it.

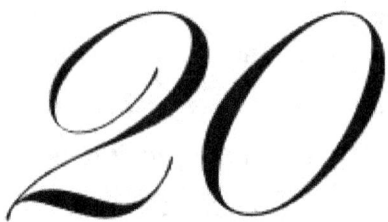

*I*ris Greenwood chimes the night. In the prime of her life. In the twilight of her soul's delight.

She takes the shapely young girl by the hand, rubbing her arm slowly from her wrist to the soft, inner turn of her elbow. Iris Greenwood follows the touch of her hand to the soft, inner curve of the girl's elbow, touching her nose to the girl's soft skin, sliding her cheek up the girl's arm, slowly. Oh, so slowly but surely, breathing one, then a second long, slow inhale through her nose by instinct, all the way to the palm of her white hand, pressing her nose and face so completely into her palm, resting it there, breathing in and out so deeply. As to what feeling this chimes into the girl's body from her

hand to her spirit, this, she does not know. She watches the beautiful woman slide her face from her hand to her wrist, then hold it there, staring at it with such a look as to be unfathomable, but taking it to her mouth gently, and placing a light and feathery kiss upon it. As to this, and the cold tingle at the center of herself, the girl does not know. As to the phantom touch of pissing at her groin, she does not know.

The beautiful older woman puts the girl's arm away, not even bothering to look, as a slice of strawberry shortcake dare not be looked upon until the silver is retrieved—she puts the girl's hand away and gets out of the truck, slowly in full length, black casual dress cloth belted tightly at the waist. Through the windshield, the girl watches the elegant brunette woman step long and lively, gliding around the right turn corner toward the driver's door. The girl looks on helplessly upon this she-beast, the creature from the night wood, reaching a strong, lovely hand to the passenger door, clicking it open as a wayward tin roof in a tornado tragedy.

What is left between terror and the girl's white skin is naught but the cool, evening air, as the woman takes her by the hand, and escorts her from the chariot seat, to the ground beneath her feet. They take hands, the two of them, strolling through the air of the evening day, to the door of the suburban house of dreams. They go

inside, into the luxurious space, the two of them. Taking their knowing walk through the algidic space, where shadows of the past and future lie in wait.

This woman pretends to lose interest in the tide that rises. In the gathering clouds of this storm that beckons. Going up to her granddaughter's room, to push through the pretense, such as it is.

*"I have to be alone with Carmen for a while. I want you to stay in here and don't come out until you see me again."* The girl answers such a quick, such a humble *"Okay Momma"* as to be heartbreaking (calling the woman "Momma" by heritage of forethought). And this, done with a voice so uniquely trembled, a melancholy so uniquely hidden, as though she were alone at the window of a house at the seashore, to witness the tragedy of waves, and wind of the stormy, sounding sea.

The woman touches little Jeannie Greenwood's hair, stroking her to tranquility, to the calm of uneasy acceptance, of what spirits have been, and of what spirits must still be. The tall and beautiful woman rises from her granddaughter's bed, unashamed to look her in the eye. Having made her understand already, what taints the rivers of blood that flow.

Iris Greenwood chimes the night. Strolling in easy confidence to her room. The room where this horizon awaits. Where pressures are built up over time. Iris walks the carpeted Hall of Antiquity, past the portraits of faces long gone, faces that gaze approvingly. Without judgment. Without remorse. The faces of women. Faces of life and death.

Iris steps into her bedroom. Unmoved by the look of fear. Inspired by the smell of it. She walks over to where Carmen sits on the bed. Standing her up with both hands. Quickly removing the girl's clothing, cloth by cloth, until she stands exposed. Young D cup breasts so fully supported in their youth. So impossibly high and pointed for their size.

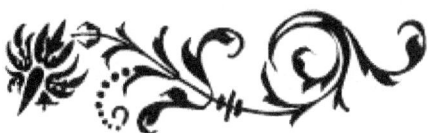

Iris Greenwood chimes the night. Standing in the girl's presence fully clothed. Watching both the girl's puffy nipples stiffen. Watching them harden from the air. Brushed to arousal by tension. Nurtured to double their size by fear.

The woman removes her clothing. By the curtain fall of the casual black dress, to the black low heeled shoes. To the big, white cotton underwear fabric slid away. To the mountainous bra silk come and gone. She stands there watching. All fertility curves and Amazonian magnificence. Breasts grown to what is not possible. Breasts that are passed from the mind of eve. From the body of Creation.

Iris Greenwood chimes the night. Stepping forward to the girl's nipples. Shocked by the spark of feeling shot through her own when they touch. Standing there. Letting her nipple rub against the young girl's. Unable to stop the grunting. The quick, breathy exclaims from the deepest woman voice. From Estros touched by Testros. From desire morphed into craving. From craving morphed into instinct.

*"I need to see you put it in your mouth,"* she says. Watching the girl reach down. Nearly brought to a quiet weeping from the inherent skill. From the sucking done to full nursing. Knowing that already, this countdown has begun. A countdown to how many more, how few of these little nursing pulls there are left that she can take.

Two.

One.

She pulls her breast away. Replacing it with her tongue, deep into the girl's mouth. Pushing back too far. Far enough to gag her. Then holding her head there. Cursing her with adjustment. Forcing her to swallow. To breathe. To learn to love her tongue.

Then instinct takes over, and the girl begins to suck the woman's tongue. Sliding up and down the length of it. With purpose. With apprehension.

The woman escorts her little captive to the bed. Watching her climb in nakedness to the middle.

"Lay on your stomach," she says. Deeply. Touching herself down below, to where the family anomaly has grown. The girl cocks of legend. The Greenwood Girls.

She climbs onto the bed. Crawling. Moving stealthily. In stealth. Placing her groin at the girls' young buttocks. Marveling the smoothness. The tight, bubble roundness she sees. With the fingers of one hand, she spreads the girl's cheeks apart. Placing the anomaly at her rectum. Trembling once already from the shock of it. The unearthly feel of it. The impossibility of it. "Oh, God," she says aloud. Unable to stop the flow of the word. The flow of this work. This work of the spirit. This work of the flesh.

Of this flesh, she pushes. Raised up high on one arm. The other at her groin, to steady the push in of the flesh. The joining of the spirit. The corruption of the soul.

She anchors herself with both arms. Every feminine muscle in her body strained. Breasts hanging down to infinity. Hips squeezed to tight, feminine form. Pushing. Squeezing. Until every inch times *six* rests inside the girl, whose breathing betrays her stress. Her fear.

The woman lies down on top of the girl. Breasts mashed heavy against her young back. Overwhelming the girl in size. In strength.

She slides her hands, both hands underneath the whimpering girl. To the warm place. To the beginning of sorrows.

She finds the center of pain. Moving her hands upon it in slow, steady rhythm. A long, hard rhythm. Without deviation. Without compromise. Knowing. Understanding that the girl's resistance is apt to be broken. Feeling her adjust her hips already. Feeling the grip upon herself loosen and tighten. Letting her voice have its way. Letting the pain come out through her voice. Stroking the girl's warmth without mercy. Without pity.

From underneath her, the girl's breathing takes new life. New desperation. So too, does the rhythm of her young hips. Trying so desperately to move. Squeezing. Unsqueezing. Squeezing. Unsqueezing. This, done in the bowels of confusion. In the agony of discovery. On the shores of a new world. In the Triangle of Needs. From her own breasts underneath her. To her groin. To the pressure in her rectum.

The woman above her presses a mighty squeeze down on her. As if by magic of knowing when. The pressing strikes a fire to the girl's groin, sent forth by the rubbing, to the feel of the great breasts upon her back, to the unfathomable pleasure in her bottom.

Underneath the woman, she jerks to be free. Trying to lift her pressed buttocks up and down. Unable to even imagine that she will not scream.

From the depths of her young soul, from her bowels, to her young womb, there explodes a power. A power that grips her voice. That rips it free. A loud, unimaginable shriek. Done once. Twice. A third time into the air.

Above her, she feels the rumbling of the earth. The sound of a woman's voice. Trembling.

Weeping.

# *It's Not Just the Blood They Crave*

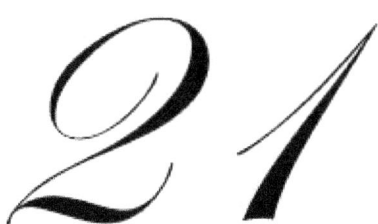

$\mathcal{W}$e both take an early departure from the bookstore in the afternoon, taking a daytime stroll in what remains of this midwinter snowfall, which continues to drift in flurries all around us, keeping the trees and the ground covered up to every horizon in a sea of winter white. We stroll in the uneasy calm to Tomorrow's Hope, braving the aftermath of trauma, loving each other enough to forego the walls of bitterness and discord, and turn instead to snowy fields of understanding and compassion.

"I should have told you it was happening to me," I say, ignoring the nosy driver in Prius silliness passing us by. For as far as the eye can see, the houses in our neighborhood are touched in beauty by the

falling snow, as scenes from an artist's dream, lifted from the canvas, or from the snow globe into our reality.

"It's your grandmother's blood," she says. "It eventually cost her her life. Can you control it?"

"I don't know. When I saw the girl this time, all I knew is that I felt a hunger inside like never before. I wanted to jump on her in the store and drag her to my office. I swear I could smell her the second she walked in."

"If it was that bad," she says, "then who's to say it's not something you really need? It's probably something you're not meant to control. My mother and my grandmother. They gave up on that a long time ago. They hunt like animals. I don't know how many girls and women they've killed over the years. It's not just the blood they crave. It's the killing itself."

"The thing that scares me, is that I'm starting to feel that myself. But it's very specific. It's a craving for these young girls. Stronger than anything I've ever felt. And it goes deeper than just the blood. Or the killing."

Anya smiles, knowingly, in the wake of an angry breeze that swirls, blowing her long, blonde hair up behind her.

"That part of it I do understand."

"What?"

"The part that has nothing to do with the blood. The killing blood. If I saw the little bitch, I'd know in two seconds whether it was blood or baby booty you were after."

"Baby what?"

"You're a cradle robber," she says. "Born and bred. Got a special craving for the young ones. Just like Iris."

"But I didn't really want…at least, I don't think I did."

"Honey, sometimes what we want to do, and what we *have* to do are two different things."

"I wanted…"

Anya turns to look at me, as if she could see what words would be formed into the fog of mist I breathe.

"I wanted her."

I turn in time to see her lower her eyes in knowing disappointment.

"I'm sorry."

"That part of us is who we are," she says. "It's what we do. These horny little MILFettes and their mothers. They think they know what lust is. I could *cum* from just slamming one of 'em up against the fucking wall."

"MILFette?"

"The daughters of these hot middle aged bitches. Or the young Mothers I'd Like to Fuck."

"It goes both ways for me," I say. "Sometimes I just want to lay on top of one of those older women and listen to her scream."

"Like Ms. Bridgeman," she says.

"Exactly like that. But I feel like she was the last "Mom" I needed. For now, anyway."

"Not me," she says. "I'm a mother lover to the last. The sexy ones, though. No bags and hags for me."

I have to laugh just a little, shaking my head at her honesty. Her audacity. "The things you say."

"You're just like me," she says. "Worse, even."

"Worse?"

A sudden, high pitched squeal and laughter catches our attention, from the direction of a nearby lawn, where two teenage girls play at dispensing violence in the snow.

"Much worse," she says.

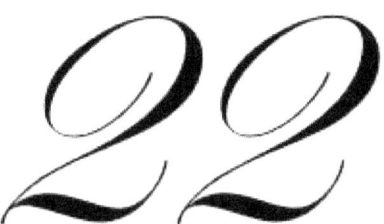

*Swiss Miss, creamy fresh cocoa, in the dairy case…*

*Yodel-ay-ee-oh…*

"How was it?"

She asks this question at the precipice of warmth—the leading edge of a warm sip from her winter mug. Whether or not the Swiss icelands have a thing to do with this sugary, chocolatey confection we sip is beyond my concern.

I join her in this little taste of winter heaven, the two of us in our winter scarves and coats, sitting at the patio table of dreams, overlooking the vast, open field of snowy, winter white behind our house.

"Well," she says. "How was it?"

"It was deeper than anything I've ever felt before. It was…a craving beyond hunger. If I couldn't have finished, I think I would have gone insane. The whole thing was like I was in a dream, *feeling* it happen, but not being able to control it. Here was a girl I had just met a few hours before—next thing I know, we're in the back seat of her car, talking and listening to music like we were best friends. And every part of me knew that she was going to die."

"How far did it go? Before you finished her?"

I glance over at the blonde beauty in the white scarf and coat to match, watching her at war with what vulgarities of these questions that beckon.

"It's okay to ask me," I say. Hoping to vent the agony of her restraint.

"Did you fuck the little bitch?"

There's my Anya.

My Swiss Miss.

"Honestly…I don't know."

"What does *that* mean?"

"If I asked you did we fuck Barbara Bridgeman before she died… what would you say?"

I watch the revelation fall over her face in all seriousness, in sober minded concentration. Her pink lips contrast in beauty with her white skin in the cold.

"I straddled her in the back seat. She was afraid, and she couldn't move. It was like she was paralyzed. It amazes me when that happens to them. And it was like I could read her mind. And I knew

that I needed for her to admit to me that she had been with her mother. It was like a sixth sense."

"Did you touch her crotch?"

I wait to see if this hilarious word she chose will touch me with a giggle.

It doesn't.

"No. And I never wanted to. But while I was straddling her..."

"I know," she says. "Those tits."

"But it was like part of her punishment. Like part of her judgment. It's hilarious when I say it, but it's true."

"Well, I can say this for her...she died happy."

My delayed giggle is suppressed beneath a smile, hidden behind another warm sip in the snow. The flakes that fall drift slowly down as far as the eye can see, unencumbered by any wayward breeze forlorn.

"Did you get naked?"

"Not at all. Only my breasts were out. Under the sweater rolled up. It was the greatest moment of arousal I think I've ever had. Because when she admitted to me that she had bounced up and down on her mother in the bathroom, it's like I could *hear* her mother screaming. It's like I could see it. And everything in me knew she had to die because of it."

"I'll bet you howled like Kim Cattrall in Porky's, didn't you?"

"And on the other end of it," I say, "were my teeth sunk into her neck."

She watches me close my eyes, and tilt my head back as I remember.

"Sorry I missed it," she says.

"I drank myself sick, I remember. I had to make myself stop."

Anya's casual look changes into a bold stare, as the next sip of her warm drink is transformed to something greater. A swallow. A gulp, maybe.

"I hope you drained every drop," she says. Deeper, and breathier than I know she intended.

"I tried to. But the blood kept coming."

The next sip of my warm drink takes on a life of its own, transforming itself in like manner as my blonde companion.

"I'll get us another cup," she says.

# Iris Greenwood Rides the Wind

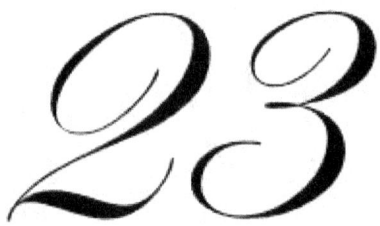

$\mathcal{I}$ris Greenwood rides the wind. On the eve of eschatology. At the front of her classroom, 11:00 am. Glancing across the chasm of space at the group of eighth graders walked in. Unabashed. Unashamed. Comfortable. Complacent in middle aged privilege and beauty. Preparing her students today for their sojourn into the joys of shipwrecked isolation, in the tale of Robinson Crusoe. Having the book already divided into sections for reading and discussion. Having the movie ready to show in three parts this week, unafraid to marry the voices of cinema and literature together. "To facilitate learning," she says. "To help make the book come alive. To make them all little experts on it," she says. "Otherwise, what's the point?"

Ms. Greenwood gazes fondly across the chasm of space. Teacher of the Year. Wondering why a certain chair lies empty today. Trying to ignore the rising tide of premonition. But at the same time, wondering how and when it will happen. Knowing that somehow, she can wait no longer for the killing of Carmen Carolini. The burial of her body in the night woods. Oh, how desperately she needs this mountain cabin scenario! Like at least seven others in times before. But they were rushed, clumsy camp killings. Seven special feasts, spread out over twice as many years. The last one, so many summers ago. Enjoying the brief, requisite grief and confusion that always sets in. So many girls gone missing in this area over the years, they would say. All of them presumed dead, they would say. Lost somewhere in those Allegheny woods. Seven little thirteen and fourteen year old beauties. Missing. Seven among the thirty nine come and gone.

There is a fortieth grave that awaits. A fortieth killing that must be done. But not rushed. Not in clumsy dismissal. Not in brute, brutal feeding. She will love this one while she dies. She will drink the life from her slowly. Pressing herself on top of the girl in full, raping missionary. Resting her anomaly inside her. Listening to her beg for mercy. For her mother. Listening to her scream the agony of pain. Of fear. Of death. Teacher of the Year.

Iris Greenwood sits in the daytime darkness of the classroom. Watching the 1$^{st}$ part of the familiar movie with distraction. Her mind lifted up past the fear of premonition, to the hunger of instinct. Knowing that they know nothing of why the beautiful teacher crosses her lovely legs. Then uncrosses them. Then crosses them again. Why she sits bolt upright and stiff, both hands at the knee, leg

swinging back and forth from the foot in perpetual motion. The anchor for the boat in the storm. The storm of raging thought, of the feel of Carmen Carolini's young body squished naked underneath her. The sound of the girl's voice in high pitched squeak, when she endures the orgasm forced upon her. Forced upon her by the soft grinding of generations, the warm pressing of preordination. The smooth and silken slide of what is meant to be lying there underneath, her weak little arms pinned tight—her healthy legs spread open wide. Every inch of the lady anomaly pushed up inside. Pushing down upon her in full weight without mercy. Listening to her cry from the agony of pleasure. The agony of fear.

The teacher uncrosses her legs a third time. Recrossing them again in like manner. Returning her hanging foot to perpetual motion in the classroom dark. Breathing a hefty, busty sigh of inner trembling. Of hidden desperation. Hearing Carmen's screams of terror in her heart's future memory. Hearing the death scream come, as she realizes she is going to die. As she gazes up into the woman's gray eyes, lightened to a shade above impossibility. Noticing the whiteness of teeth blared. Watching with shock and disbelief the sharpening growth of two.

Iris Greenwood rides the wind. The wind of her desire. The vibration of a young girl's constant screams, tearing into her body. Flooding into her soul. Activating her animal instinct. Her feeding mechanism. The transformation of her face into unearthly beauty.

Unearthly terror.

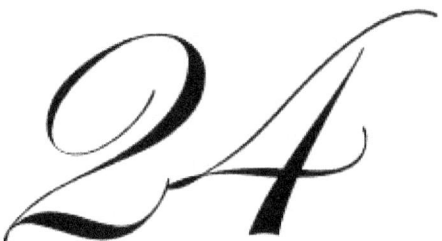

$\mathcal{O}$ver the course of generations that flow. In the gathering of the lust for blood. The beautiful teacher is shocked awake from the security of the daytime dark. Where young minds are on a journey to their future.

Iris looks on with as much bravery as she can find, when the Principal opens the door in false civility. When the door swings open to the familiar eyes that stare. Eyes of a mother's contempt. A mother's seething rage in check. The eyes of where Hell hath no fury alike in kind.

The beautiful teacher stands tall in Amazonian stature. Allowing the bosom to cushion her fall. To protect her dignity in the fall from grace. She braves the entrance of Death and Hell before her, the two strange men of authority. Men that she chooses not to fear. Men that she despises.

The beautiful woman braves the otherworldly terror of their calling. The implications of what they say. Words that announce to her classroom that her time has come and gone. That her days of freedom are done.

In front of the eighth grade, the men of authority take hold of the beautiful woman without fear. Without remorse. Unafraid of the power she wields. Feeling the rush of capture and conquest. In the periphery, the lovely teacher sees the fearful stares. The wide eyed confusion on the young faces. Seeing the future newspaper flash their eyes in premonition: *"Teacher of the Year Arrested for Molesting Student."*

The teacher speaks her last words to them in dignity. In a breath of reassurance. Somehow feeling the need to see them comforted in this hour of grief. In this hour of tragedy.

In the wake of this crashing wave ashore. In the rise and fall of the crashing, sounding sea. The teacher is guided by the men of authority through the door of her past to the present. Not seeing the look of endtime scorn passed between the women. Between the mother and the teacher captured. Guiding her in statuesque splendor dressed down, the elegance of extreme beauty unadorned. Strolling her past the Principal who gazes in lying eyes, the other teachers who wear their masks of fungalooga. Their masks of public servitude.

False faces of cultured civility. Glimpsing the young female teacher, hands over her mouth, wide eyed with disbelief, as your mentor is carried away from this life. As the exotic bird in flight is captured. As the tiger whose eyes are burning bright, glides away in fearful symmetry.

The teachers watch the brightest star fall from the heavens, dying in a fiery flash of light. Dying in a blaze of glory. She strolls in beauty among them as a mystical creature captured in the forest shade, brought forth in wild dignity to the clearing. To showcase inspiration on display. Divine creativity made known.

They watch this woman leave the school against her will. Pulled along in elegance. A tiger washed forward, in the floodwaters of her impending demise.

Iris Greenwood rides the wind. The Winds of Eschatology.

Jonathan Lovejoy

# In the Throes of

# Another Winter

# Snow

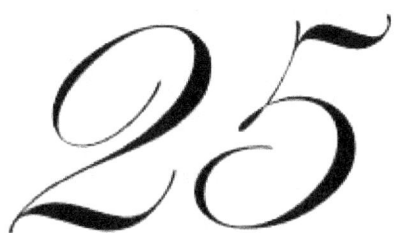

raving this winter storm of envy. The pastor's wife and her beautiful daughter. A girl in the fullness of teenage youth— curves of innocence not yet fully grown. Fourteen or fifteen thereabouts, so sweet and brunette in innocence known. In this, the return of winter snow, a month after other snows of grief have flown. More deeply emboweled in the pains of winter we are, and bitter cold down to the marrow of bone.

The pastor's wife and her beautiful daughter, inside our suburban house of dreams. So carelessly engaged upon our invitation for a visit, to share smiles and fungalooga cake therein. I am exhilarated into nearly a pissing floor, when I watch Anya slap the taste from the

sweet, sexy woman's mouth out of the blue, staring so vehemently at her daughter's face iced cold in fear.

*Shut the fuck up* are the tragic words I hear, spoken from the mouth of my Dear, my dearest, to the woman red faced in confusion and fear. *You're so fucking horny you stink of it,* I hear my Anya say, in the throes of another winter snow. *Pastor's wife,* she says with scorn. *Pastor's whore.*

*Why did you slap me? I don't appreciate that,* Mrs. Repression says so diligently in her cause. Pledged to love her enemies, believing this to be a test from God. Oh, but such a test it will be, Sweet Honey, on the eve of Eschatology!

Escorted up the stairs in pleading, these two, upon realization that no, there is no physical strength they possess, there is no strength of will that they have, there is no force of Destiny that shall lead them past the two of us to the doors of freedom. Oh, such a wickedness of violent struggle it was, to see this cultured woman break down past the hypocrisy of love, past the phoniness of respect, past the ruse of politeness shown, to ball her fist in fury, and begin to strike my Anya so hard upon the shoulder as she tried to pull away. This, while I had held her daughter immobile by the throat, as she screamed *mother stop fighting please—please stop fighting her*—and this, choked off by my hand in instinct, which would not allow me the privilege of remorse, nor even the echo of mercy and compassion.

All that I can do is breathe the deep throes of a lust even I have rarely known, as I hold the daughter tight so nearby their escape, watching Anya subdue the angry woman with such little effort of muscle and bone. Watching her turn the woman around and stand behind her in full control, exhilarated to agony by the scene of the healthy hipped woman in her sweater and faded jeans, winter coat fallen to the floor, held immobile by a beautiful blonde woman no bigger than she. Holding her tight from behind, until the woman's rage grits her teeth, until we hear *let me go you fucking witch, let me go goddamnit,* said with such effortless aplomb, with such angry passion as can hardly be imagined, as if she is suddenly furious with the object of her fervent blasphemy.

We round the corner into the upper room, two by two, with me guiding the young brunette in from behind her, my hand still around her throat, led forward by the spirit of Iris Dove herself, knowing already what I'm going to have to do to the pastor's daughter. Behind us, I hear the aggression of years of repressed rage still releasing itself, like the volcanic eruption that pours forth in such an unbelievable stretch along the pendulum swing.

*"I'm gonna call the police on you two witches I swear. It's too late now, you two have had it."*

Yes we have, my dear.

And we're going to have it again.

"Take your daughter's clothes off," Anya says.

*"I won't do it!"*

The woman screams in the wake of another violent slap. And then another. And then another.

"I said take off your daughter's clothes."

The woman's refusal is cut off by the threat of another slap, held in mid air by the blonde beauty in tow. *I'm sorry honey,* are among her last words spoken, as she pulls the girl's clothes off down to her bare skin.

"Now take yours off," Anya says, "down to your underwear."

"Please don't do this," she says. "I'll give you money, I'll give you anything, I swear I won't call the police. I won't say a word. Please."

I watch Anya's look soften.

Lovingly.

"You want us to let you go," she says. Stepping close to the woman. Intimately to the woman.

"Yes, please," she says, glimpsing fearfully at her naked daughter.

"Then come closer. I want to feel how badly you want us to let you go."

"I do want it. I do."

In the energy building, in the rising that doth not subside, she leans forward in the knowing kiss to her captor's lips, trembling in the full, pressing kiss, a kiss remarkable for its latent heat, and energy of raw, unrestrained sensuality it displays. The fact that fear is the world's greatest aphrodisiac is on full display, as the woman kisses Anya with genuine enthusiasm, and a lust that cannot be manufactured to such a degree. It is as though she is allowed to unleash this unexplored desire in a cause; the cause of saving her daughter from whatever tragedy there is that awaits.

When the kiss is done, the two stand together like lovers, gazing into one another's eyes, the woman wiping the tears from her own, sniffing, gazing hopefully into the blue eyes of her captivity.

"We can go home now?"

"I'd like to let you go," Anya says. "But you know that I can't do that."

"Yes you can. I'll take my clothes off if you promise me you'll let us go. Promise me?"

Anya stands so close to the woman of like age as she, matured perhaps seven years beyond. Matured to perfect female sensuality. Aged to perfection.

"I promise."

Jonathan Lovejoy

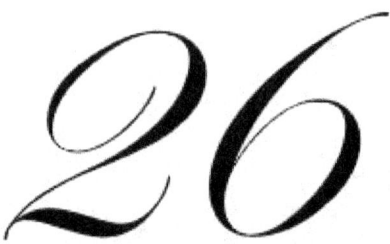

*I*n the wake of promises made, in the aftermath of false hope conceived, the young girl watches her mother begin to take of her clothes. The pastor's wife slowly, deliberately slides out of her pink turtleneck sweater, fabric in perpetual suburban cable knit pattern, taking the sweater off in perfect speed and cruise ship vacation rhythm, exposing the tight, pink shirt underneath, where secrets are revealed in the key of D minor, in such impressive contrast to the flat, immaculately curved waist below. She pulls the t-shirt out of its tucked in place, out of the tight, faded blue jeans, barely taking her eyes from Anya, sliding the t-shirt over her head unashamedly, to reveal the frilly white bra and soft cleavage underneath.

I watch Anya's expression become more melancholy, instantaneously more somber, as the woman undoes the tinkling buckle of her belt, unbuttons her jeans and slides them down with slow, determined purpose, revealing a shape that could not disappoint, as the prototypical set of motherline hips bubbled and spread outward to infinity. I wish to speak upon it, but dare not disturb my lover's impromptu ritual, and what spark of fire and delight must be ignited within.

"Do you want me to take off my bra?" she asks. Pitifully.

"Honey, that bra was made to be worn. Leave it."

"Okay," she says. Nodding her head, glancing again at her daughter in my clutches. "Now can we go?"

"Come here."

In her frilly, silken bra fabric and tight, French cut underwear cloth, she steps forward in pleading to her captor, to her mistress, taking her by both hands and staring her in the eyes in silent pleading, a silent plea, in pleading silence for a reprieve.

"Patricia, I'm sorry. But I can't let you leave."

"But why? Please tell me why?"

"Because…"

In the sempiternal drift, in the pause to infinity, the sum total of the woman's public façade, and secret debauchery flashes before her eyes.

"You and your daughter have to die."

On the heels of the woman's new pleading, behind her begging "oh no" is built the long syllable of a woman's voice on the edge of a full, weeping cry. A cry of the condemned.

"It's alright," Anya says, hugging the woman so tightly as she cries. Then I watch her begin to undress, removing her white pearl cashmere open cardigan, tight white t-shirt blouse and black jeans, to reveal the toned, Amazonian magnificence beneath, a physique of nearly Olympian athleticism, but with the tiniest waist possible, to accent perfectly rounded, teardrop hips and buttocks. An upside down heart in purity of shape and form, and appropriately so, as the opposite of mercy is her own heart's way and means of survival.

Fully topless, and in black underwear string, her bosom upon the same key as her captive, she turns the crying woman around to face the scene of her soul's dread. Standing close behind the woman in full strength activated, holding her arms tightly to her sides, staring at her closely from behind her.

"Jeannie," she says. "Do what you have to do."

Held tightly from behind, the woman weeps bitterly in silence, as I step away from her daughter, and undo the first button on my white blouse.

$\mathcal{O}$lympian truth is soon revealed to our little world, as I pull my unbuttoned white blouse free from my long skirt in darkened fabric. The Fear of Certain Death accompanies the first part of the truth held up in the largest bra this woman has ever seen or imagined, as I lean down to unzip and remove both of the black boots. I do not look the crying little thing in the eye, as I unzip and slide my skirt away, to reveal the second part of the truth, which is Fear of the Grave, in a body curved beyond what is reasonable to fathom. The black, thigh high stockings are done away with, as I glimpse the young girl in the periphery, who gazes upon my features

body, to tingle the anomaly I possess, until I am able to feel it grow from the squeezing at my groin and the pressure building up in me from deep inside.

With little patience for her naivete, I order the girl to the bed, telling her to lie on her back, climbing onto the bed and to my knees at where her legs will soon be spread. I open her legs gently, gazing every inch of the young girl with craving and hatred, understanding only that her pain is my pleasure, and her suffering is salvation for my soul. I slide closer to where our paths must meet, taking both hands to my groin, to pull the swollen lips of myself apart just so, to push my anomaly further out than it already is, exposing the enlarged, pink tip of it, causing the woman to cry out hopelessly *she's a virgin please… she's a virgin…*

Oh, but what virginity is this do you mean, Dear Woman? Is it the chastity of the mind? Surely not! For what girl of age in the modern day has not browsed the computer screen in private! This, the end of the age, dear Lady! This is Autumn of the White Woods, the death of Innocence, the death of Chastity in the mind of every little girl at the end of time!

"I need to see her punished," I say.

"Just say the word, Baby," Anya says.

"Sit her mother at the edge of the bed."

Anya complies quickly, forcefully guiding the woman to this place.

"Lie across your mother's lap," I say.

"Oh, my God," Anya says, putting her hand gently to her own lips in mild shock.

The naked girl climbs over the mother's lap, lying flat across her mother's thighs, her buttocks raised slightly from the position.

"Punish her. Punish her until she cries."

Hopelessly, in the frustration of her life's power come and gone, the woman proceeds to spank the girl, mildly moving her hand from one side to the other with determined skill of restraint.

"Do it right," Anya says. "Or I will."

And what mother could refuse this last leap, this last grasp at protecting her daughter from this strange, end of the world harm that threatens? In the energy of a mother's fear, and the fury of a mother's protective scorn unleashed, she lays into a stream of hard, steady blows to one side of the girl's tender skin on her backside, doing this with determination and vigor, until the girl's voice flows out a loud cry on its own, past the barrier of her resistance and beyond. I watch Anya staring at the scene in a rapt amazement I've never seen on her face before, as she places one hand upon the front of her underwear cloth, to anchor herself against her body's rapid rise and fall toward devastation.

The bare breasted mother is determined to break down this barrier, readjusting herself, delivering another stream of hard, steady blows to the girl's bottom, concentrating on the single space of deep red, seeing the girl's skin begin to spot itself towards a bruise. And when the girl's voice falls, when she is pushed beyond the cliff of her resistance, the mother can hit no more from the numbness in her own hand, saying...

"Give me a hairbrush."

Anya can only stand mesmerized, her mouth open in her rapt amazement gone epic.

"I said give me a *fucking hairbrush!*"

The woman screams deeply, seeming to frighten Anya into motion, causing her to hurry to our mirrored dresser, and remove the classic wooden punishment tool in waiting.

"Mom please, please don't…"

"Shut up! Just shut up, *please!*"

And I watch Anya put both hands over her mouth, as the mother proceeds to try and burn the girl's skin to fire and bruises, sending her to a place beyond weeping, to where crying is but a signal, a symptom for what pain and agony are surely yet to come.

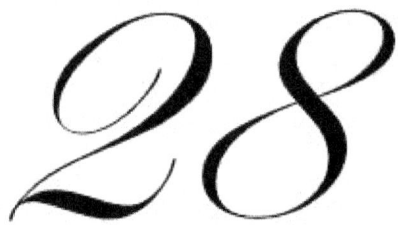

The two of us watch the girl's suffering, burned in the fires of our own craving, suffering as we watch the mother cut her daughter's white skin to blood. It is her last, desperate call for help, her last scream above the drowning waters, before she is pulled down into the cold and dark of the briny deep. We watch her do this without ceasing, until the girl's flesh is cut and blackened, and the wood is stained with blood. The mother's rage gives place to the sorrow of the ages, as she regrets the pain she has given her daughter, the day she first spoke to us, and the day her mother caused her to be born.

As I help the broken, battered girl move away from the lap of blue and black fire burning, Anya takes the hairbrush from the exhausted, weeping woman, tossing it to the floor, pulling the woman up in reverence, staring at her as if she were a beautiful thing to be observed, a glorious event to be watched, an uncovered treasure to be savored and stored.

"I'm sorry you have to die," Anya says. Kissing the woman again as she sobs and weeps, then holding her close, looking at me over her shoulder, as I stare down at the devastated young girl on her back.

"Don't make me watch her do it to 'er. Please don't make me watch it."

"But I have to," Anya says. "We'll watch it together."

Anya shushes the crying woman, slowly ushering her around to where she sees my heavy breasted self at the girl's groin, pushing what can in her mind only be something I am holding in my hand against myself. Pushing it slowly into her daughter's waiting self spread open, the woman howling the word "no" while she shakes her head, watching me shake my own head once in disbelief at what pleasures have shot into every inch of my body, as I lay down on top of the grieving young girl, staring into her eyes as a jaguar in the Amazon woods, laid atop of an unlucky fawn in the evening day.

I can feel my anomaly's remarkable growth continue inside her, as it pulls my hips down to a deep and powerful squeeze, causing the girl to cry out once in pure pain, to join in duet with her mother's as I watch the girl's face twist in suffering from the death of Chastity,

and feel her young body tighten up against mine. My Triangle of Needs chimes the dreams of Caitlyn's blood, calling out from my breasts, to my bowels and my womb, to gather my entire being up as one with the universe, causing me to hold my head back as my hips grind slowly under their own power, feeling the spirit of who I am begin to transform me into a creature of pure instinct, bathing the fullness of my breasts with what power they possess, causing my vision to haze in the periphery, as I open my mouth, looking down at this girl in a new light, seeing her eyes widen in terror at what she sees.

Her screams are at a new and fever pitch, to match those of her terrified mother, who has become the embodiment of fear itself, as she witnesses the lightening of my eyes, catching a glimpse of the sharp pointed truth in my open mouth, as I stare at what part of her skin this truth will rest upon.

And when the woman sees my eyes, when she sees the sharpness of my teeth extended, she looks at her mistress for hope of sanity, seeing her blue eyes phased to the self same whiteness of winter cold.

In a predator's instinct unbridled, I clamp down upon the girl's neck in the sharpness of truth unrestrained, as she lies underneath me screaming, causing cataclysm to erupt into my body in ways I have only imagined before, joined in matrimony to my lover's hunger unleashed, as she holds on to the screaming woman's breasts from behind, while the Truth is buried deeply into her neck in another endtime cataclysm.

# Nearby the Northern Timberlands

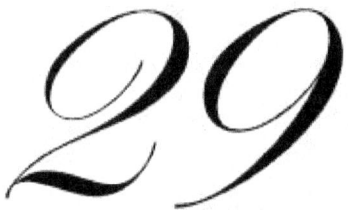

The truth lies buried deep in the Minnesota snowfall, across the frozen, windblown landscape of the North Woods. More than one hundred victims lie in wait for the Resurrection, more than one hundred souls having departed this for their eternal reward. So few of these bodies may be reunited with the righteous souls that have left the earthly plane—those that left in righteousness when their lives were taken. These will be transformed in the twinkling of an eye, and shall be resurrected from the grave, and they shall be caught up with Him in the clouds, to meet the Lord in the air. These are they which will be raised incorruptible, soaring beyond the northern tree canopy, higher than the mountains, beyond the sea of clouds in day or night, until the surface of the ground is a far and distant memory.

Past the lunar light, the souls of these victims fly, off into the far reaches of the second heaven, whereby the passing stars and galaxies declare the glory of God, on their journey to the shores of the Third Heaven.

This is one of the out of the way places. The tiny, two bedroom cabin home, nearby the northern timberlands, north woods isolation in the winter cold.

The mature woman in the mirror is gripped by wonder. Brushing the makeup onto her face, barely needed. A face unburdened by fungalooga smiles and laughter. Wondering whether or not she chose her ridiculous life, or whether it chose her. Living in the same small, log cabin looking anachronism of a house her entire life. Following her mother's footsteps from restaurant to restaurant, waiting tables. Having neither the luck nor the ambition to do better. Cursing the day that she was born because of it.

The woman prepares for four o'clock twilight. When the winter afternoon hours presage the fall of night. She prepares to brave the darkening of the winter landscape again, as seen from the inside of the busy restaurant diner. Enjoying the years of perpetual worship she has received for her beauty. Dark blonde hair stylishly pinned, hoop earrings dangling. *"My husband's a long haul truck driver,"* her enduring explanation. Gold wedding ring worn in formal declaration to a lie. A lie born from the truth from a quarter century ago, when the long haul truck driver was alive. Before his life was taken in screams and blood.

*I hate it when you leave,* her mother says. *I wish you could stay here with me.*

The mature woman gazes a divine reflection in the mirror, more extraordinary than her own. Standing directly behind her, looking barely a few years older. Drawing so many wide eyed stares and compliments from all who have been made aware. Mother and Daughter.

The older beauty stands close behind the waitress. Not looking into the mirror. Staring directly at her daughter, refusing to speak again.

"Momma, what are you doing? I can't take the night off," she says. She tells her mother to move, so that she can leave for work. This, answered by a knowing, good natured stare only.

The mother's tight grip is a warning. A warning that a toll must be paid, if the waitress wishes to pass her by. Even though the waitress is in the mood to work. To leave the dreary confines of isolation for a shift. To breathe the fresh air of civilization. Of freedom.

The waitress knows that if she wishes to pass, a toll must be paid. So, she presses her lips to her mother's. Briefly.

The disconnect is the sound of a kiss. Ringing a chime in the mother. Causing her to hold her grip and stare.

The bathroom mirror holds a reflection. A reflection of reality. A reflection of a mature, beautiful woman, pressing her face to another for a second kiss. The mirror holds the reflection of these two. A moving picture of a kiss. Of a woman turning her body to the other beauty, wrapping her arms around her in full. A deep, lover's kiss extended in secret. Eyes closed, loud breathing through noses. The

older woman moaning so deeply from the feeling that rushes through. Mouth trembling from the power of a kiss.

From the beauty.

# 30

A sixty two year old powerhouse of a woman, she is. Born in the Ukraine, raised in the same northern backwoods spirit she brought to this country when Veronica was twelve years old. Cuckolded by an older man when she was only fifteen, and left with the consequences to bear. When her mother found out that Enya was pregnant, that she had allowed herself to be taken in by a man's lust, she did not speak. She only swung the back of her hand to Enya's mouth, in a strength more overwhelming than what is even possible for a man. Sending Enya reeling halfway across the room, then leaping upon her suddenly, before she could barely recover from the

first blow. Holding the pregnant young girl up with one hand, hitting her twice with the palm of another. Slapping her around the room, literally, until she was nearly senseless, with only the sound of her own screaming in her ears, and her mother's word murmured in Russian, *"I'm going to beat it from you."*

Enya was never allowed to go to school another day after that, and the bitterness from her mother prospered, until the life of the little bastard was threatened from the time she was born. Little Veronica Lepardovsky is lucky to be alive, to be sure, being that her grandmother punished her so often and so severely that she once broke her arm. And this rage threatened to eventually blossom into the truth of the blood that flowed in their veins, when Enya's mother spoke the words in Russian, *"If that little bitch sasses me one more time I'm going to kill her."*

And were it not the company of her kind, young Enya might have dismissed the comment as dark allegory, as a threat to vent the pressure of bitterness grown. But the look in her mother's eyes when she said it. The calm, determined sanity in her voice. The years of behind closed doors beating of both Enya and her daughter. All of these were the sum total gathered up and presented as one, to warn her that her mother's natural bloodlust was crossing the line, to where her own granddaughter was simply to become one of many. One of the many backwoods killings already achieved in secret, where the taste for little girl's blood tormented her dreams night and day.

So what is Enya to do, then? What is she to do, when the feeling for her daughter blossoms beyond merely the maternal instinct, into an emotion that cannot let this happen?

And so, literally in the dark of night, there is a covert young Russian woman who braves the winter cold of travel, seeking to flee the hands of Fate turned dark, and the looming threat that hangs like a terminal illness over her daughter. Enya braves this cold in the dark of night, to take little Veronica away from the northern winter woods of the Ukraine, to leave her mother to the task at hand, which is to add to the list of missing women and children, and to dig the shallow graves on her own for the rest of her life in rich and ice cold Russian soil.

Enya Lepardovsky stands at the door of her cabin. Remembering with such lustful fondness the feel of a kiss. The warm, soft feel of her daughter's lips, the taste of her daughter's tongue pulled so deeply into her mouth. Enjoying the look of frost gathered into the winter air like smoke from her mouth. Admitting to herself that there is the feel and taste of another that calls to her.

The name of Enya's granddaughter calls to her in the evening day. On the edge of the approaching night. She closes her eyes, to remember the feel of a beautiful young blonde facing her naked in her lap, her tight and toned teenage body trembling, while her rounded breasts were pulled so deep into Enya's mouth in sucking. Anya Sugar Rolls, is the vulgar nickname spoken to her mind. To her spirit when she remembers the sweet taste sugary kiss, the lollipop licking sweetness of her nipples in permanent, perpetual protrusion.

The young girl that was given to her by the dark angels that serve her purposes in life.

First, a child of seven, two years removed from the killing of her father she witnessed when she was five. *"A little seven year old temptress,"* Enya had spoken to her daughter, as they undressed the beautiful little girl, and both licked and sucked her flat, undeveloped little breasts without compromise and without reservation.

Oh, what Hope doth remorse decry in futility, dear woman! What sociopathic and sadistic chimes do ring! Oh, how often in the night, has your body rung the bell of this belle departed for lands down east, nearby where the storms from the grieving Atlantic ocean are blown in? How many times, Enya Dear, doth the strength and yellow haired, blue eyed beauty of her soul call to thee upon the night wind? What is it, dear Enya, that you know of the taste of a vampire woman's blood? The purity, the sweet twang that rolls like wine over the palate? Why, Dear Enya, do you know that as surely as your daughter drives the early evening miles in the snow, why do you know, that your life has led you to this point to bear, that you and your daughter must soon fill yourselves on the taste of your granddaughter's blood?

# 31

*H*er job is to serve her mother's lust. To lift it and carry it like a pile of wood in the snow. Since she was a little girl in the Ukraine, she has been the object of her mother's divine affection, her sublime determination. Even in the dispensation of pain, there was pleasure. The pleasure of many shudders and tremors, many shakings and earthquake rumblings, in full blown mother daughter lust—carried over even to what her mother called "a ridiculous marriage" to a long haul truck driver. That *"stupid son of a bitch"* she called him, when the two of you were so glad to rid him of his iron and saltine blood, and burn him alive in his truck, where Fate

granted the two of you an explosion to boot. And this signaled the fiery beginning of the end for you and little Anya, when the fullness of the Enya mind hath blossomed.

Veronica Shier, a.k.a. Veronica Lepardovsky, rides the snowy miles to the busy restaurant. Not necessarily hating her hours on her feet, gleaming pretty white teeth in the hungry fools' faces. Glad for the brief respite taken from the hauling of the wood in the snow. Remembering the magic her mother wields over her mind and body like no man ever could. Remembering why she is going to be late for work. The way that her mother had gripped her bottom in full strength as they had hugged in the bathroom, lifting her up onto the sink in gentle roughness with her legs open.

The way that Enya had taken time in steady, determined deliberation to take both their breasts out of the dress tops unbuttoned. Pressing them together—reconnecting the kiss. With her daughter's legs spread open, her dress slid high up her thighs. Veronica remembers her mother's anguished, determined expression beyond pretense, beyond Hypocrisy's reach, when she raised her own dress up just high enough. Pressing the warm front of her underwear cloth against her daughter's to the rising of a blazing heat, and to the pre-shuddering of a tragedy impending.

As Veronica drives hurriedly to her failed place along the timeline, she remembers the cushion of her mother's breasts mashed against hers. The look of hopeless agony upon her mother's face, the brief shaking of her head and looking away as she tells you to grab

her backside, but spoken in the vulgar vernaculate, the vernacular still heavy burdened by the Ukraine, and the seed of depravities passed down from the mind of Eve. With her phantom member fully grown, with her place against her daughter fully established, she drinks in the beauty of her daughter's face as she thrusts once hard and mighty against her, sending such a shock of revelation and reminder into her daughter's body.

The mother stops once but to breathe, to establish herself for the load that must be given, and the burden of it that must be borne by her lovely daughter in full. Enya thrusts again a second time, another mighty blow against complacency, against the memory of ordinary lust, crumbling under the weight of an instinct too heavy to bear, concerning the words to her daughter *"I'm going to have to fuck you."*

And this, she proceeds to do, in the power of her phantom member grown, and the front of her swollen self slammed repeatedly against her daughter's. With her daughter propped up on the bathroom sink, with her legs open in her waitress dress raised up her thighs, the mother proceeds to become a conduit, an instrument of the Sapphic, that spirit of Amazonia unbridled, as every hard thrust carries her forward, faster and faster toward the high dive cliff in her sight, running without fear in the full spirit towards it, like a white mare in full battle charge on the open plains of war.

The daughter must give in to what heavy pounding this is, holding on in deep kisses and support, hoop earrings dangling the force of motion, her body vibrating from both the pounding of her strong mother into her, and the gruff, animal bellowing sent deep into her body, muffled by the kiss locked in perpetuity. Veronica remembers the beginning of the end of her own sanity, a cry of the damned she prays will not happen, answered by her mother's sudden release of the kiss, and the involuntary howl of fear and agony into the brief space around them. The hard tension that breaks into her mother's body, causing her to shake and tremble helplessly into the aftermath of another explosion, leaving the daughter spared of this pain, at the precipice of falling without going over, while the blissful chimes ring in her body from head to toe.

In full strength, in the power of fierce loyalty and unbridled passion and fever, she kisses and licks the beautiful woman's face to ease her suffering, every inch of elegant cheek and soft lips exposed, moaning loudly and deeply in time with her mother's gruff loudness, the long and continuous moaning in the voice of woman, to carry the melody of another woman's deeper voice of devastation and ruin.

Veronica drives the snowy miles. Remembering words spoken in the aftermath of trauma. In the throes of breathing to live. Words to the affect—*we have to find Anya. We have to kill her...*

Veronica drives onward in the snow. In the shadow of the evening day. Wondering where it is that her beloved daughter could have gone.

# American Vampires in the Riviera

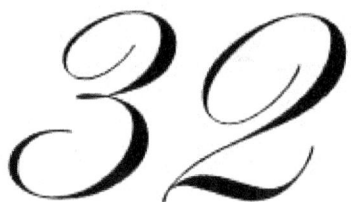

Our winter vacation in the south of France would normally not bode well for the French countryside, were it not for the fact that we have satisfied this hunger for now, to lay it dormant through the passing of another season. We rest our weary souls now, unguilty, on the cold beach along the Riviera, but far away from the prying eyes that stare.

"In the history of God's Creation," Anya had said, her mouth hung open as if she had never seen me in a bikini before. And when I had tried to laugh it off, to deflect her attention elsewhere, she had stopped me cold, saying "Just let me look a minute, Jeannie." I had to stand there in the hotel room embarrassed, lips tucked in over a smile of pure humiliation, while she gazed at me slack jawed from top to bottom.

"You might be one of the most beautiful women in the world," she says.

"Anya, please don't."

"I know you're embarrassed by it, Honey. But face facts. You've got a face like Miss Universe, and a body like a busty pinup queen. To tell you the truth, I've never seen anything like it. In pictures or real life."

"Well, I have. I was raised by it."

"Oh yeah, you did tell me about your mother. Is she really as gorgeous as you?"

"She's an older version of me. With bigger breasts."

"Bigger? For God's sake, *how?*"

"It's a real condition we have," I say. "There's a medical term for it."

"What? Boobalitus mammalia?"

"No," I say, trying not to laugh a little, adjusting my white sun hat in the mirror, though our time on the winter beach will hide our bikinis under our coats and scarves.

"Come on, what is it? Breastoplasty, what?"

"My mother is a real world, honest to goodness example of something called *macromastia*."

"Macro...what?"

"Macromastia," I say. Turning around from the mirror, to shine the big, low riding headlights in her eyes. Giant, swinging cleavage, it is, held in place by the boulder holding black bikini bra cloth sling.

'Macromastia," she says, staring at her high, rounded D minors in the mirror.

"Extreme breast growth. It's sometimes called gigantomastia."

"Giganto— " She snickers loudly, covering her mouth, looking at me in the mirror. "I'm sorry."

"It *is* funny. I know how ridiculous I look."

"Well, masto, giganto, whatever. All I know is if Wonder Woman had Kim Kardashian's ass and Milena Velba's tits, she'd be you."

"Who's Milena Velba?"

"The end of the world."

On the beach, the waves of the crashing, sounding sea rise and fall at the shore, pushing a great sheet of water high up onto the sand. A great distance away, we can see the leisurely milling around of a few lost winter souls like us. Whether they be French or no, is unknown to me as I stare with interest across the great space of sand, listening to the music of the gulls that drift and dive in noticeable numbers, as if waiting for the appearance of something unknown upon which to feed. Anya is engrossed in one of her vampire novels, reading another addition to the infinity of failed attempts to capture the reality of us in literary form.

"Where do they get this shit about us burning up in the sun? It's just the opposite, for God's sake. We don't even tan in the sun. Our skin hardly even gets *warm* from it. They always show us as these cold-blooded monsters, flying and fucking all the time."

"They got the second part right, didn't they?"

"Yeah, we do fuck a lot," she says, still focused on the bloody goings on steeped in myth and legend. "I wonder what the world would say, if they knew that we were real."

Somewhere in the distance, I can make out the figure of two teenage girls walking slowly along the shore. A twinge pricks every nerve in my lower body, causing me to rub my right leg once against the other leg it is crossed upon.

"Sometimes, I wonder," she says, closing the book and dropping it into her blue carry bag. "I keep having these weird premonitions. Like something bad is gonna happen."

"When don't you have weird premonitions? You said the same thing in Hawaii, remember? After we got that woman on the beach. She was so fucking stubborn. I was glad to finally shut her up."

"I had almost forgotten about that."

"That's because she was just a kill to you. But I enjoyed every second of her suffering. I'll bet she wishes she hadn't left her husband now."

"I wonder who her husband was," she says. "How he reacted when he found out."

"I couldn't care less."

"You know what we should do? We should move here. Get a house in the country. Do what we need to do in perfect isolation. Put the fear of God in the French countryside."

I don't answer, gazing at the image she just burned into the theater of my mind, of the farm girls and farmer's wives that would suddenly begin to disappear for a hundred miles in either direction.

"Do you really think we'll be able to go home... without sampling some French wine?"

I return my gaze to the distance, at the minions of merriment under the gulls at play. Wondering in my heart if this part of the world is protected for now, from the American vampires in the Riviera, and if their bloodlust has been satisfied well enough for the remainder of the winter season.

# 33

Over the French countryside. Across the gathering of every city. These are signs of the times. Mother daughter perversion is pervasive and mean, in the beauty of corruption and sin. From the European landscape and beyond, to the shores of where I was born and bred.

I see the light-skinned black lady lawyer of the northern city, the yellow skinned ethnic beauty, so deeply engrossed in the signs of the times we are in. I see this forty five year old lady lawyer with the

rich and successful husband, three daughters of like ethnicity born. I see the teenage rebellion of the yellow skinned beauty in the middle, endtime insolence and disrespect allowed to prosper to alarming levels.

I see the lady lawyer ensconced in her pride, end of the world self-importance nurtured and grown. Unable to endure the daughter's resistance of her yellow-skinned beauty. The arrogance, the disobedience of fifteen year old maturity. The father's absenteeism, his workaholism allows for no intervention. No compassion for the grieving mother.

The lightskinned lady lawyer is at the end of the proverbial rope. Having exhausted all means of modern punishment. Every restricted curfew. Every loss of privilege. Every confining to a homework ridden weekend. All of these have failed to curb the daughter's sass. The light-skinned bubbliness of a personality pushed beyond the limits. Beyond the limits of mother daughter civility.

In the brownstone confines of the city. Beneath the skyscrapers of latter day prosperity. A rich and successful husband is out of town. The oldest of three daughters is away on a skiing trip to Aspen. The youngest daughter is in sleep over heaven, in the gathering of other little pre-teen flowers, in the home of Asian mother daughter iniquity unknown. End of the world iniquity un-shown.

When the husband is away. When the oldest daughter is away. When the youngest daughter is away. The middle daughter is all alone. A deer in the clearing grazing naively. A tragedy of unawareness grown.

In the wake of another argument. In the burning of ground zero. The mother hears the words of a doorway open. Words of a four letter vulgarity spoken in teenage anger. Without apology, remorse, or regret. This word is spoken to the light skinned lady lawyer's chagrin. Spoken to her angry delight.

A confirmation scene, where the woman is made aware that the daughter said it. And she meant it.

A grabbing of the daughter's hair. A grabbing of her arm. Escorting the mature young girl to the mother's bedroom. To the queen's chambers.

The daughter is unfamiliar in this wilderness. In these waters of her mother's contempt born and raised. Exploded to the fullness of itself. The fires of hatred allowed to prosper.

The mother locks her bedroom door. Standing in the shadows of the forest leaf canopy. Beneath the surface of cultured civility.

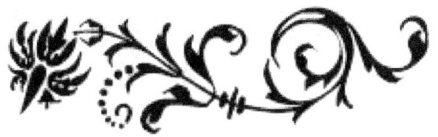

The lightskinned, beautiful woman stands still in judgment. Watching her angry daughter take off every stitch of her clothing. Until the angry and shapely young beauty stands yellow skin bare. Bikini waxed and clean shaven for her mother to see. Big, dark areolas and nipples puffed out upon ripe, rounded breasts yellow and firm. Breasts that play their melody upon the key of F major. A prodigy among young girls. The envy of them all. The desperation of every boy and man. Yellow brownest, bubbliest, bustiest cheerleader in the school. The only yellow skinned young beauty in a sea of

white. Set up by Fate for a prosperous future. A ride of Preordination's Track. Daughter of a rich man. A rich woman.

The rich woman goes to her mirror dresser drawer. Retrieving the turmoil in silver and chain. Silver and shackles in miniature.

She pulls her daughter's hands behind her back, locking her wrists down in the cold. In the cold and unbridled truth against her daughter's skin.

The lightskinned lady lawyer disrobes from top to bottom. Gazing the daughter's eyes that stare. Watching her feign bravery. Watching her struggle to hide the shock. The inner awe and amazement. Having never seen her mother completely nude. Unnerved by the hang of the yellow breasts a key higher than her own. By the width of the hips exposed in full. The tiny, fleshy waist revealed in magnificence. Curved into hips spread out to infinity. The curves of a former athlete softened by time. Grown to Amazonian proportion. Hidden from the world. Bras and business suits. Panty hose and pumps. Small waisted, big curves hidden. Repressed in waiting.

The beautiful light-skinned lawyer slaps her daughter hard. To ring the chimes of her future. To wipe the smile from her face. The giggle from her spirit. The insolence from her soul.

She grabs the sides of her daughter's head. Pressing in full strength. Yelling assurances, that this four letter vulgarity will never be spoken at her again. Watching the smile fade properly from her daughter's body. Seeing it gather up in defiance, and trickle down

her yellow face in a single tear. To signal the turning of a frown. The ignition of fire tinted blue and black.

The ethnicity of her youth and upbringing colors the mother's speech in this anger. In this rage unleashed. Assuring the daughter that she is aware of her own greater prettiness, greater breast beauty, greater prowess about the waists and hips. Words spoken without censure. Without pretense to cultured civility. Insults about the daughter's ethnicity. Supremacist insults passed down the timeline from her white mother. Words legislated out of public society. Imprisoned deep into the human heart.

The nude mother goes to her closet of dreams. Returning with a fiberglass cane. A blackened rod of purpose. Thin and flexible heat ready to be given.

She proceeds to stripe the front of her daughter's breasts without mercy. Watching her façade begin to crumble. Watching the waves of pain crash at the shores of resistance. Watching her daughter's mouth finally open in anger, to hear a cry of pain delivered in rage. A scream of pure agony.

She slips the rapid whip in rhythm, to send the anger on a trip to bountiful. On a journey toward transformation.

The daughter's hopping up and down in pure pain delights the mother to no end. Causing her to have to continue. The hopping is always the signal. The signal that pain thresholds have been reached. When the daughter's sobs have reached the breaking point, when there is no more resistance left to cry, the mother puts the cane away. Taking the girl roughly by the arm, throwing her roughly to the bed. Climbing heavily on top of her. Taking her daughter's big breasts into her mouth, sucking the nipple hard enough to cause bee sting

agony. Hearing the girl scream in a different tone. A tone of fear. Of sorrow.

She plays this secret rhythm upon both her daughter's nipples, until apologies begin to leap forth. Promises of attitudes adjusted. Swearings of behaviors come and gone. The mother lays these bee sting sucklings hard upon her daughter's nipples, to listen to her scream. To listen to her spirit go dark. To feed the roaring blaze of endtime fires tinted blue.

When the daughter is broken down to sobbing. To weeping. The lightskinned mother climbs up to her yellow skinned beauty's face. Whisperings of a mother's affection. Of disciplines that must be complete.

The mother receives a kiss of contrition. A deep, desperate drowning in sorrow. Sliding her mouth off her daughter's tongue in a loud, sucking kiss. Returning to her daughter's nipples in a flicking of the tongue. In a gentle nursing of pleasures unbridled. Tongue skillfully bathing the daughter's breasts in softness. Turning the daughter's old resistance into a new craving. A new instinct.

The mother slides her tongue down the daughter's golden yellow-skinned beauty. Down to her naval. Resting deep kissing and lickings upon it. Moving in circular momentum downward. Down to where the daughter is waxed and clean shaven for the mother to see.

The mother attaches to the daughter's chastity in sucking. Amazed at the girl's immediate, hard shake and tremble. Switching

between lips and tongue. Kisses and licks to infinity. Until the daughter's defiance begins to flow out of her voice in moaning. Loud, breathy moans of warning. Still bound, unable to escape. Legs open, held in position by her mother's strength. By her mother's skill.

The woman hears the moans begin to grow. Reaching out for a third kind of scream. A cry for a reprieve. A cry for redemption. A cry for mercy.

The mother hears the daughter's voice in outcry. In the explosion of high pitched sound. A scream unique to every woman. The Pandora Scream. The scream of exhilaration and inner amazement erupted. Risen into the sky like a geyser untapped. A soprano song to the rafters. A call to the heavens.

The mother locks herself down to the daughter's chastity. In violent flicking of the tongue. Pushing her daughter past endurance, to where only begging and pleadings remain. Pushing her to a place of agony. A place of fear.

The woman releases her daughter in mercy. Taking a soft trip of the tongue, back past the naval, to the brief and gentle nursing again. Back to her daughter's exhausted face. To her awestruck expression. Asking the proverbial question, as it pertains to motherhood. To the possession of a mother over her daughter.

The mother feels herself in involuntary motion. Positioning herself to her daughter's groin. Pressing. Grinding herself to it. Wrapping her arms tightly around her daughter. Laid heavily on top of her in missionary. The daughter's arms still shackled behind her back.

The mother feels her hips go to motion. Feeling the rising and lowering of them in hard, steady rhythm. In fear of what tragedies must befall her body. In regret over the taste of forbidden fruit. Unable now to stop the trains of momentum, and the agony of bitter wormwood.

The woman must raise her head in the pounding. Turning her gaze to that Great Looking Away. Somewhere beyond the windows and walls of secret, backward and forward along the timeline, somewhere between earth and the stars of the second heaven. Feeling her body pound itself, along the course of Predestiny, a preordained track of causes and effects.

The mother hears herself echo her own mother's voice without effort, to reference the name of *God* and *Holy Jesus* in fear and pleading, until her daughter witnesses the tension in her face break, and sees her expression turn to shock and disbelief, as she feels the energy gathered in the center of her body explode outward, trembling every inch of her great buttocks in rippling waves passing through, traveling up her spine and into her great breasts, as her voice does the siren cry of the banshee, where she must take a breath, and release the siren cry in full, until it crosses over into a weeping, and a cry to her Lord and Savior to have mercy.

In the aftermath of grieving. In the aftermath of trauma. The lady lawyer rests nude upon her daughter. Breathing the scent of her contrition. Absorbing the energy of a spirit broken for all time.

The mother lays still and quiet upon her daughter. On the eve of eschatology.

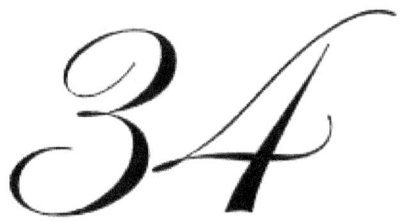

*Dunque io son…*
*Tu non m'inganni?*
*Dunque io son…*
*La fortunate!*

*(Then, I am…*
*You're not deceiving me?*
*Then, I am…*
*The fortunate girl!)*

*My* soul is lifted upon the wings of eagles. Carried aloft, past the walls of this great opera house, swept along by the rising chords of manic ingenuity, sprung from the well of inspiration that is The Farm Girl's Opera. From our cool, but scenic respite on the isolated, winter beach at Saint Tropez, through our last day flight

north to the City of Light. From our awestruck, wandering stroll past the chandeliers and the golden columns in the grand foyer, to our time in the red and gold horseshoe shaped auditorium of splendor hearkened from another century in time—I am enraptured by the divine ingenuity of what I see and hear, art of such extraordinary beauty as to be immortal, to lend us ear to the voice of God in laughter and pain, and the grief of the Almighty disguised in joy and song. It is the only opera I truly love, which is the case for so many who claim allegiance to the operatic stage, but are unable to escape the pretense of superiority, and those who look down upon Rossini's masterpiece. I listen to the music skip and prance from places beyond Inspiration, which is only the hope and prayer of Genius, who struggles to manufacture the truth in God's Creation.

We are unable to allow a year to pass, without attending this opera somewhere in the world, being that it is the happy sound of our coming together, by the whim of Fate herself. I am swept up and carried along these velvet sounds, where the timeline beckons the heart of memory. I am transported back to 10 years ago, to the entrance hall of the American Opera House in Virginia.

I had tried to get my reclusive mother to go with me, having no stomach for any other date or company of any kind. But true to form, Betty Greenwood had refused, and so I find myself at the Virginia Opera House alone. Whether or not I am there to hear the opera, or to hear the blood rushing in my ears when I spot my next victim— this, I do not know. But already, I am a product of my birth, a twenty three year old hunter (10 years ago), imprisoned by a bloodlust that started when I was sixteen. Being that luck has no morality, I have been protected— from the first little girl I lured away from the park into the nearby woods for a fatal stroll, through high school and college, into my first year as a graduate student.

In the winter of my 23$^{rd}$ year, I am drawn by the magic of Rossini's opera, to hear what miracles of melody there are to have made this opera immortal, and what sublime sounds could follow that bright, pristine comet fire of an overture. I remember that the soprano's bosom outdid her singing by a mile, though it did not matter at all, as both were encapsulated by the strains of manic ingenuity from the orchestra. What divine blessings are the opera divas of the world privy to, that they create such an aura of irresistibility?

After I watch and hear the lively finale burst forth in such a splendid farewell from the end of this age, I walk out among the stunned and confused crowd, delighted by their own bewilderment at what divine madness has come and gone, and of two hours spent in echo of the Great Music Hall, overlooking the shores of Heaven. The

rising hunger in my blood calls to me, as a wolf strolling through a heard of sheep, waiting to hear the call to strike. But there are none that cry out to me as an opportunity given, as life bestowed to me with as much generosity as is given to the birds of the air. Somehow I know that I will find what I need to live, to avoid slipping away into madness.

In the craving of bloodlust born and risen, I walk frustratedly to wherever it is that I have parked, to drive home alone in the Virginia night. After an eternity looking for my lost car, I find it somewhere on the outskirts of chaos, seeming to be somewhere other than where it was three hours ago. And suddenly, three elements in the flow of time come together in the space around me; the touching of my hand to the car door, the feeling that I am being followed, and the sound of a woman's voice echoing somewhere in my brain.

"Excuse me," are the words I hear spoken in kindness and beauty, as I turn to see a blonde woman of extraordinary appeal, with features of absolute and unmistakable prettiness to behold. "I'm so sorry to bother you, but do you go to the University of Virginia?"

"I'm a grad student there."

"So am I."

And thus begins this convergence of two paths, this merging of two wayward and lonely tracks into one, where I learn that she had seen me many times walking the campus alone, but had thought I was a professor or a drama school student or music major. I watch

closely, this beautiful blonde woman smiling and gushing genuine
enthusiasm at finally meeting me, though it be in an opera house
parking lot in the dark of night, knowing within myself that
somehow, her appeal is otherworldly, and her gladness to meet me is
as real as every strand of color in her long, golden blonde hair.
*Sharon Tate* is the tragic name whose face echoes through time, as
the level and manner of beauty this young woman is that I see.

From the heart of memory, I am pulled back into the Paris Opera,
beside the beauty 10 years matured, having grown into the fullness
of herself on the top side of thirty three (which is thirty four, nearly
thirty five) as I lag almost two years her inferior. As the heavy basses
in the orchestra begin to skip and play, beneath the voice of the
soprano hopping about gleefully above them, I am again reminded of
the joy she infused into me that night, when we found ourselves
away from the restaurants and the cafés and the malls, sitting alone
together in our car, enjoying two of the biggest cheeseburgers we
could find at a drive through, both of us so relieved to find someone
else with such a huge and unholy appetite.

What travelers along the road of life are these! Two tigress
hunters in white, striped the color of death, whose eyes burn white
from the ire of unfed hunger within! I see these two, laughing,
talking, engaged in the normal human feast of joy and brief leisure,
to quell the raging instinct inferno, to make the pain of our living
tolerable for another season. And somewhere in the swirl of our
touch of happiness, I hear the edges of sorrow approach like a

gleaming sword on the battlefield, when beauty speaks the words in false mocking, *"what if I told you that I was a vampire?"*

From the heart of memory. From the look I had given her in the silence of shock. The quiet awe of disbelief. From this look given to her over our first time together, to where I am burdened by it again a decade later. I look away from the doings on stage, not of my own volition, letting the sound of the duet voices carry my soul to the rafters, where I take my lover by her spirit hand, and look with quiet awe and disbelief into the midst of paradise, into the misty eyes of alabaster and blue.

# 35

To fuck her daughter. To be fucked *by* her. These are the heart and soul of what devastates the mind, body and spirit of the Enya psychology. This, as she lies pinned underneath the beautiful woman who is her daughter, arms pressed so tightly to her sides. Legs open in missionary, having had her strength dominated in grieving. Lying there, with the understanding that there is no atheism, no resistance by conjuring, no power under Heaven to block the realization of what force must rise itself to completion, of what course must devise the destruction of her world, no power under Heaven and the light of the winter Mountain Moon, that can stop what must happen to her body. This, as she is locked in, as her daughter's arms hug her body

tight in Valkyrie, pounding her groin in perfect and consistent fashion, to where the only answer is that yes, there is a God, and he is going to destroy her both body and soul.

This, as her daughter hath found the God and Jesus rhythm upon her, to drive a wedge slowly between her and sanity, until thoughts of tonight and tomorrow begin to fade, and time slips forward and backward into eternity. She lies there, a prisoner of the Enya mind, as her daughter drives the message home in the sound of bare skin slapping, of bodies clapping together, in movements too far beyond inevitability to stop. This, as she readies herself to endure the howl of the lycanthrope, though brought forth from the spirit of bloodlust and vampirism in feminine form and beauty.

She lies there, afraid to voice the names of Divinity that torment her mind, that threaten to force her to have to cry out for the Redemption she cannot have, the absolution she cannot receive. Enya lies there, underneath her lifelong servant of dark intent and motivation, unable to fathom where such pleasure hath borne, and to wherefore doth it hearken and flow. Enya lies there, held prisoner by the spirit of what tragedies must befall, the culmination of her life's

work, the monumental end of her days as the purveyor of human blood, and as one of the greatest killers of womankind ever born.

She lies on her back in suffering, her eyes affixed upon that Great Looking Away, upon that place so far off, past the walls of her bedroom, somewhere past the crystals of nighttime snow that falls. And in her last grasp at what sanity there is to know, Enya sees upon the theater of her mind the death of Anya, the demise of her progeny a generation removed, sensing the heart of her screams in her mind, and the taste of every drop of her blood in her body.

Upon this, the rhythm of the angel's chorus sings into she knows not where, and she must begin that pitiful howling, taking the quickest breath she can, so that she may express this calling in full into the night. The names of Divinity pass through her condemned mind and body, as the angel of darkness caresses her being without mercy, causing Enya to cry out pitifully in weeping and wailing as her sanity abandons her in full, and leaves her to plead and beg her daughter for mercy.

Jonathan Lovejoy

# Iris Greenwood Rides the Wind

# 36

_I_ris Greenwood rides the wind. Somewhere in the flow of time and history. Knowing that the spirits that have granted her every gift, these have come to collect their debt. To take back what privileges they have given. These are the privileges of blood and freedom. The privileges of freedom and blood. Tried and convicted in a court of law, under a mountain of public shame. Having watched the girl she trusted look her in the eyes without remorse, and point at her in the courtroom. As the woman who did things to her. Things spoken in somber detail. So that the community at large can be forced to watch and listen to the Truth. The truth about what churns beneath cultured civility. The truth of what secrets lay buried in the human heart.

Iris Greenwood rides the wind. In the aftermath of conviction. Pulled out of society as a female predator. A beguiler of young girls. Having watched breathlessly for the rising tide of accusers to come forth, but to no avail. This lone accusation, this whispering voice in the wind. The Carolini girl. Rescued by the arms of Fate. By the whims of Destiny. Rescued from the tragedy of an early death. Death by fear and pain.

Iris Greenwood sits on the floor of her prison cell. Behind the locked door of Hell. Understanding the power of premonition. The power of what is meant to be. The beauty of wealth gathered, transferred to her daughter before she was taken. Transferred to her granddaughter in trust. Assets they could not touch. Seven figure wealth whispered into being over the years. Wealth bestowed by Fate alone. Gifts in gold and emerald green. Gifts in the glow of diamond. Monies passed down to her beautiful daughter. To her beautiful granddaughter.

Iris Greenwood rides the wind. On the floor of her prison cell. Naked. Her mouth covered in the blood of what must be done. Her grieving body having been fed to completion. Having no pity, no remorse for the dead body of her cell mate. For the naïve mother of two come and gone. Lying still and quiet in the dark. Unseeing eyes laid open. Eyes that stare in empty judgment. Eyes that stare in mocking. Eyes that look without sight, at the condemned naked killer

of women and children. Drunk upon the last wine of her privilege. The last rites of her sanity.

Iris Greenwood rides the wind. On the eve of eschatology.

Jonathan Lovejoy

# The City of Light

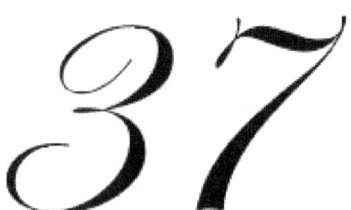

"$\mathcal{I}$ hate this fucking city. It makes me wish I were dead."

At the top of the Eiffel Tower, I gaze at Anya in genuine shock, wondering how she could draw such a conclusion over the City of Light. The lights of earthly progression glow all around us as earth stars, stretching far off into the privileged lives of places unknown.

"How can you say that about Paris?"

"Paris is no better than any other city in the world," she says. "They're all infested. Crawling with two legged vermin."

"So that's what you mean when you say you hate this city. You don't really hate the city at all."

"Part of me wants to set up shop in the country somewhere over here," she says. "We can spend the rest of our lives making as many of these French bitches wish they had never been born."

"Or, we can just end it all. Never bother to go back."

"You mean jump?"

"Why not?"

"Because I want to live," she says. "And I want to be happy."

"But how can we ever be happy, Anya? Doing what we do? Being who and what we are?"

"Because they deserve it. Every little mother *fucking* one of them."

"But sometimes I feel like I can't judge them. Especially these secret mother lovers I can smell a mile away. Both of us grew up doing the same thing. Are we any better than they are?"

"The morality of the executioner is not in question. We merely obey our life's calling."

"And what is that calling, Anya," I say. Turning back to stare her in the eye.

"To kill. To feed. To strike the fear of *God* in the souls of the condemned before they die."

I turn back to the view of the city lights twinkling in the distance, unable to deny the images of the teenage girls I saw, walking the winter shores of the beach at Saint Tropez.

"Are you still going to quit Barnes and Noble?" she says.

"I'm going in one more time. To say goodbye."

"And then what? Not that rose garden."

"Maybe. It's been in me for a long time."

"Is that where we're gonna keep the bodies?"

"Absolutely not. There has to be one place in my life that's not stained in blood."

"Is that what I am to you now," she says. "Stained in blood?"

"You know I didn't mean you." I say this looking back at her again. A quiet, fiercely determined stare.

"They're gonna hate you for quitting, you know. You and me were good for their public image. *'Lesbian Couple Finds Corporate Success With Barnes And Noble.'* They would have been the envy of every big company in the world. They were going to blast our pictures everywhere. We would have been invited to people's houses. Company executives. Politicians. Gay rights activists, which might have included singers, actors. Who knows? With that Miss Universe face of yours, and that literary body…"

"None of that was gonna happen anyway. I couldn't have done it."

"You're not quite the people person your grandmother was, are you? You're Betty Greenwood's daughter, alright. You're headed in the same direction. But that's not what you're really trying to do."

"What?"

"You're turning from it," she says. "Trying to start denying what you are. And the harder you try to push it away, the more it's gonna become a part of you. I watched you good the last time. I saw you wishing you didn't have to do it. I saw the pain and the guilt on your face. And I also saw the surrender. I saw you give in to it in sorrow. Like you couldn't have stopped it if you tried. And the funny thing is, between the two of us, I'll bet you're a bigger killer than I am."

What words spoken work dark magic in the brain, to flood fear down to every particle of the soul?

"That's right," she says. "That part of it comes straight from your grandmother. And we both know what she was. You had no pity for that girl. No remorse. The more she suffered, the more you liked it. When she was spanking her daughter's little fat ass, I saw you close your eyes in ecstasy. I saw it, Jeannie. You've got an end of the world lust, Honey. And you might have the biggest *girl cock* in the world."

These last words, she speaks softly, deeply into my ear from behind me.

"You can't hide from what you are in a rose garden."

As if summoned upon the breath of the word "garden" breathed, the sound of two female voices chimes in, enchanting us by their native tongue, of which Anya and I are both so conveniently, so inevitably familiar with, knowing enough of the language to say that we can speak it, with smiles and apologies for our "bad French" impending. As the mother and her young daughter giggle and chatter past us, to take their own frigid, nighttime look long overdue in their lives, Anya looks at me with the assurance of an angel of prophecy, with nary a smile, nor any allusion to the whims of chance or coincidence, devastating me with a single look that yes, this is a dark and end of the world calling to obey, and that the tragedy of human existence is Fate.

# 38

The lady lawyer remembers the scream. The scream of inevitability. The scream of chastity dying. This, at the end of the day, when her case is at last prosecuted and won.

The lady lawyer straps the leather carrying case closed. Unable to disassociate. Unable to distance herself from the feel of the straps pulling into place in her hand. Remembering the pull of leather straps about her hips just the night before.

*So our bond can never be broken,* she says. *So we'll have something special they'll never be able to take from us.* This, in the hotel room of dreams. Where she needs to live at times in brief, to better focus on the end of a hard case. This time, in the hotel where the jury is hidden.

*I'm going to need some company tonight,* she tells her husband. *I want Kimberly to spend the night here. She'll love it.*

The lady lawyer wonders if she is unique among women. That she must strap the member to herself when she is alone. To stroke every inch of it as if it were a part of herself. To watch her reflection partake of this diversion. To marvel the curves of her own body, as they contrast with the realistic member strapped on. To focus upon the big, yellow breasts exposed—not touching them at all, lest she spoil the self visual. To stroke the member in rapid motion in private, until the motion is involuntary. In the likeness and manner of a man.

Expression of this lifetime envy made known to herself in secret. Observing the best of both worlds in the mirror. Wearing it for so long at times that it becomes a part of her. An extension of her. A protrusion. A secret level of futanari perversion. Fantasies displayed in vulgarity on her computer screen, where women express this lust in members that function. Depravities spewed forth from them, in the manner of a man. Closing her eyes, imagining that what she wears can provide such expulsion. Grabbing on to the mirrored dresser for support. To anchor herself for the trembling. In the earthquake shaking of her body.

The lady lawyer remembers the visual. The fantasy of an Asian mother who possesses a real member, and how she expressed herself upon her daughter. Her soul's reality displayed in fantasy. A sign

given to her, she believes, of what part of her life's calling must manifest at last. What spire to rest upon the top of this tower built.

As the lady lawyer leaves the empty courtroom behind, she is burdened by the heart of memory. By the memory of a scream. In her mind's eye, there lives the visual of her fifteen year old breast queen. Skin in like golden beauty as she. Infusing the daughter with sensitivity over the exotic coloring. A tragic vulgarity spoken in the heart of perversion. *Momma's little nigger bitch*, she says. *Hold 'em up for me.* This, she says to her daughter without reservation, as her daughter sits at the edge of the hotel bed. Holding both her own breasts up. Watching her beautiful, strong willed mother tap the member hard against both of them. Against the front of them. As to what feeling this hammers into her spirit, she does not know. *Put it in your mouth,* the mother says. *Slide it in until you choke on it.*

The lady lawyer remembers the tears that rolled down her daughter's face in grieving. But not the sorrow of weeping. This, the tears of choking alone. The phantom cry of a phallic choking. Streams of tears and spittle fallen down.

She takes the member from her daughter's mouth. Lest she tremble prematurely. In the agony of endtime arousal, she lays her daughter gently on her back. Climbing on top of her in full. Two sets

of enormous breasts pressed together. Mashed together. Pushed out
in roundness at the sides of
their bodies. The mother and the daughter.

In fear, the daughter knows to open her legs. The mother raises
up, to see the Autumn of the White Woods. To see the death of
Innocence. Gazing down at the member she holds. Placing it at the
door of what is meant to be. Watching her daughter's loveliness in
tension on her face. Watching her grimace from the pressure tip
pushed in. Holding it there. Leaning down to her daughter's breasts.
Pulling one of them high up into her mouth. Releasing it in a loud,
sucking kiss. Watching it fall free, wobbling back into roundness in
repose. As to what devastation this is to her soul and spirit, this, the
daughter does not know.

Her mother lays down upon her in full again. Pressing their
breasts together a second time. Staring her daughter in the face as she
pushes herself deeper into her. Watching the discomfort turn to pain.
Lowering herself all the way down, to where her and her daughter
are cheek to cheek. Feeling the daughter's fingers grip the flesh on
her back. Feeling every muscle in her daughter's body strain.
Steadying herself for what must be. For the final part of this journey
into madness.

The mother squeezes her hips forward. Pushing her member in
violence through the door. The door of what was. Of what can never
be again.

In the evening day, the lady lawyer remembers a scream. A cry of pain.

Of Death.

# 39

The mother and daughter we leave behind weigh heavy on my soul and spirit, high above the waters of the grieving earth, nearby the stars that decorate a moonless night. I stare out the airplane window into the void, unable to see anything beyond the faint glare on the window, and a blinking red light on the airplane wing, having traded seats with Anya when we first boarded, moreso to be away from the crowd of Hellbound souls than anything else. The stench of brimstone is heavy in premonition, corrupting the air around me in putrid warning of things to come. I know better than most ever born, that a ticket to ride Heaven's Train is not bought and paid for with good works and righteous living, as some who will be sent to the Lake of Fire will someday soon discover.

I have never felt more burdened by the confines of my moving cage, these iron bars of Fate, than I feel at this moment along the timeline. I understand more than ever now that life is nothing more than a series of preordained, predetermined events, and we move along our paths as having been chosen, rather than ones who have chosen of our own free will. What we think we have chosen to do in life was already chosen for us before we were born.

I think back upon our last hours in Paris, being driven by the kindhearted, pretty young mother and her quiet little twelve year old daughter, who had been too enamored with the two of us to not speak to us on the tower. In fluent English with the heaviest French accent imaginable, the dark haired, doll faced thirty something insisted that we accompany her voluptuous self and her little stringy haired Rebecca (though her name was Sharon) back to their humble little house far on the outskirts of the city, *"to eat some real French cooking and have a glass of real French wine,"* she had said, which made me have to resist the urge with every part of my strength to glance at my blonde companion.

I can remember feeling as though I had no control over who I was at that moment, like I was being lifted from another path chosen, and set on a new course that was chosen for me. *I'm in France,* my mind says to me in the old, gray Honda, steering wheel fascinatingly on

the wrong side, going through the unfamiliar streets until the lights grow fainter and farther between, until eventually we are on the outskirts of the city, speeding along through the mysterious dark to who knows where, to the home of the friendly, talkative Amazonian, short haired brunette, who truly bears no resemblance to shyness, nor pretense to apprehension and fear. What I can feel is the desperation of loneliness, a woman abandoned by her husband, whom she says with good natured boldness, *"because he got tired of my hand across his face."* And I see the daughter giggle in submission to the truth of it, that this big boned beauty battle-axed the poor man to death.

The woman is every bit the farmer's wife. Pale, pretty features, unaided by makeup—with large, dark eyes, the source of her effortless appeal. A thick, shapely body fit for the strength needed in rural life, and time spent on a farm raising cattle. *I can never find anyone from the city who will come to visit me,* she says. *What, are they afraid I'm going to keep them a prisoner in the barn?*

The audacious amusement, the amusing audacity of her question draws a curious stare from me. I look this strong, pretty woman up and down with admiration, and a desire to know whether or not she was a child when she fucked her mother. *Motheress*, is the word that begins to whisper in echo in my ears, to assure me that I have been called and chosen, and placed here by Fate, Destiny and God.

The voice of Katerina, the farm mother's strength, still echoes in the forest of my memory. Somewhere in the muffled roar of this

airplane that carries us to freedom, I can hear the roar of the angry Amazon, who screams in unfathomable rage as she is held by my blonde mistress, unable to overpower her, though the farmer's wife is a woman of strength and durability.

The woman's screams of fury dominate the theater of my mind, which shows me a visual of myself in the farmhouse, removing my top and my bra to let my breasts hang heavy and free, as the little twelve year old French girl looks on in confusion at her mother, not knowing fully what fate it is that she must suffer.

I am unable to hold myself in check from this feeding, my hands trembling in need of this fix, and I spring topless at the frightened little girl, tearing at her clothes while the mother watches in fear and rage, as her daughter is being attacked by the crazy, big breasted American woman. Burdened by the pain of pure instinct, to relieve it I can only clamp my teeth into the little girl's neck the second every strip of cloth is ripped from her body, feeling the relief course through my veins like medicine, in ecstasy that rings a chime, in the midst of her mother's angry screaming, where I am laid full and heavy on the girl topless with my black jeans still on, pinning her motionless on her back to the floor.

The heavy hipped, thunder thighed woman calls on every ounce of strength she has left but to no avail, while she watches her daughter twitch and kick underneath me. The anger in her voice is suddenly frozen away, when I raise my head up to take a breath, and she sees the sharp pointed truth bared in white stained with blood.

And she is suddenly held captive by the universal reality, that *the types of fear are many, and uniquely distinguished.* Among these is the Fear of Death, which touches the outer portion of her skin like a winter breeze, and sends revelation down into the center of her body.

"Iris," Anya says. "Fill yourself, and then come to me."

And I lower my head again to the woman's pleading in her native language, *"I implore you, please let my little puppet girl live."*

Anya holds on to the woman so tight, watching her from behind, feeding upon the aura of despair and hopelessness flowing from her adventurous spirit conquered.

I am pulled suddenly from the theater of my mind by the flow of violent energy building, across the aisle and one seat forward, when a busty stewardess with an inch of makeup caked on leans forward to a passenger and says in a light French accent, *"Just because you are black, does not mean we have to take this shit from you,"* erupting the scene in the loudest slap I have ever heard, a pop that fills the enclosed space, followed by the pulling of hair by both women, the black woman of middle aged sophistication and substance standing up to continue what her slap started, with no passenger brave or stupid enough to go anywhere near this end of the world anomaly;

which is a mature, sensible looking, yellow skinned African American woman falling to the floor underneath a glamorous white stewardess, whose made up face was twisted in rage when they fell. Anya stands up as the only one brave enough to show genuine interest, swearing to herself out loud that she will "knock the shit" out of anyone, man or woman, who touches them.

And this inner promise, I watch her keep, as she squeezes past the battling women when they have been at war for at least half a minute, to violently shove two stewardesses away who have come to throw water on this fire. Anya's sudden burst of violence snaps me back to the farmhouse in the dark, where Anya fights to contain the struggling farm mother, who has just watched her twelve year old daughter die a fearful death. In the heart of this vivid memory, amidst the smell of human flesh and burning brimstone, I stand up in full, topless glory, the demonic whiteness of my eyes displayed, and the sharpness of my teeth in blood. *Yes,* Anya says to the woman, as her screams fade, while the fear in her eyes grows ten fold. "*Accept it. This is your punishment for your lasciviousness. Your lust. You think I don't know? You think that I believed we came here to eat French pastries and drink wine with a twelve year old? Honey, you were calling me like a backwoods banshee. You wanted me to rape you. You wanted me to do it while my friend watched it happen. Iris, tear off her clothes…*"

In the ease of what strength I am given, I make quick and easy work of her country flowered dress, to expose the shape of her unglamorous underwear in the cold, this healthy hipped, perfect breasted farm woman, stripped to her underwear is a work of art I must witness to completion, to *not* touch an inch of her plain bra and underwear cloth that struggle to hide what lies beneath, that cannot enhance breasts that are hopelessly flat, nor hide hips that are hopelessly fat. Pear shaped perfection, this is, the shape of fertility uncovered in the fall of night.

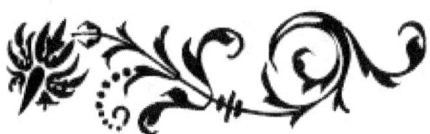

*"I can smell your cunt,"* Anya says. Sliding her hand down the front of the woman's underwear cloth. Squeezing. Causing the woman's frozen expression to squeak out the smallest part of a scream that will never come.

*"Iris,"* Anya says, *"Tear off her underwear."*

This, I do. While Anya holds onto the nearly naked woman, listening to her grunt in fear.

*"Iris,"* she says. *"Unhook her bra."*

This, I do. To complete the woman's total nakedness, with Anya standing behind her *completely nude*, as she has been since the beginning of this woman's tragedy.

*"Iris,"* she says, one hand around the woman's throat, the other locked between her legs at her groin. *"Bite her breasts. Bite her breasts so I can cum."*

This, I do. Clamping onto the heavy hipped, small bosomed woman's breast in uncompromising intent, as the woman begins to cry out in fear and pain, accompanied by the cry of a backwoods banshee, echoing across the French countryside in the dark.

Jonathan Lovejoy

# Iris Greenwood Rides the Wind

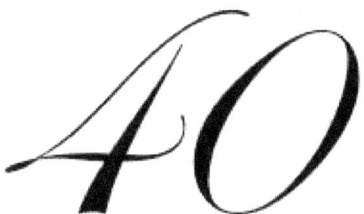

*I*ris Greenwood rides the wind. The winds of her sanity come and gone. Having struck fear in the hearts of every inmate, as word spreads like an Armageddon fire. *A female prison guard was attacked in her cell, when her cellmate was discovered in death and blood. The female guard was overpowered by the crazy teacher, who clamped down on her neck like a vampire,* they said. A second, third, then fourth guard it took, to subdue her screaming in madness to the floor. *She looked like a monster,* they said. *Her mouth was covered in blood.* Teacher of the Year.

In solitary repose, she waits. In the dark of nighttime solitude. Feeling the edges of a former life slipping casually away. Perceiving only the rising of a bloodlust within, greater than any she has ever felt. Having lost the stomach to digest any other nourishment for life. Knowing that she must feed again soon, at the end of her seventh month. The approach of the eighth month, the approach of a new season. A new feeding.

She bides her time in solitary. Embracing the pretense of likeability, with the flow of guards by her vicinity. Twenty three hour lockdown, a daily escort to an hour of recreation. An hour of relief from her exile. Teacher of the Year. Drawing looks and stares of curiosity and bewilderment even now. Extraordinary beauty, they say. How can a teacher do what she did to a female student? Then how can she do what she did to her cell mate? A teacher of the year? A mother?

Iris Greenwood rides the wind. The winds of a gentle breeze that blows. A breeze wafting through the fences of maximum security. Barbed wire above. Forests and fields of serenity below. By the return of a hunger. Wondering when it will be, and where will

it happen, when the short, shapely brunette guard is taken. In the coming eighth month of her confinement.

*"Iris,"* the pretty young brunette guard calls. Unafraid to approach the docile beauty. Convinced in her heart, that what has happened in the woman's life is an anomaly. Nothing more than a series of unlucky events. Surely, the young girl she was accused of molesting was lying. Surely, Carmen Carolini misinterpreted her teacher's intentions. Misinterpreted her affection as inappropriate. Clearly, this is how a woman of such shapely and statuesque beauty wound up in jail in the first place. They don't know how sweet and kindhearted she is. She probably went crazy from pure fear, when she had to kill her cell mate. The woman must have threatened her in some way. The guards she attacked were being overly aggressive. Attacked her while she was pumped up on adrenaline. Just one bad luck incident after another, this poor woman. Someday, she will earn her way out of solitary, and maybe she can mingle with others. Maybe she will return to her studies. Perhaps even to teach others while she waits. While she waits for time to forget. She is over fifty. But how can that be, when she barely looks a day older than thirty three?

Iris Greenwood rides the wind. Adrift from her isolation at the high wire fence. From her view of the forests and fields beyond.

Teacher of the Year.

# Anya Aphrodite

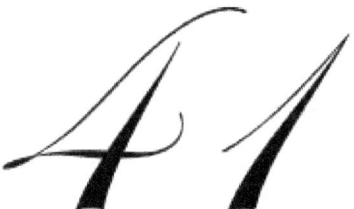

$\mathcal{M}$emories of warm blood on a cold night swirl around me, as we cross the boundaries of New World air space, where it seems the endtime landscape is buried in ice and snow. Our brief respite in chilly Saint Tropez and Paris had only been an echo of the winter we left behind. What we thought were the last flurries of bygone snow have resurfaced in angry reprisal, to greet our return to the states with an icy hand of winter warning. I notice that even as we land, there is only the cleared strip of asphalt that tells us we are headed for safe ground, as the airport terminal itself and the sea of parked cars in the distance, along with the surrounding landscape are all covered in new fallen snow. But we land safe in rolling, dramatic fashion, cushioned by the knowledge that we have been called and chosen to live, and go forward from here to the next girl or woman who is destined to die.

But before we leave the plane, we are all trapped aboard for an extra half hour of brutal, self important nonsense, as law enforcement gathers and surrounds the outside of the plane as if ISIS terrorists are inside. And even while lights flicker and flash red and blue nearby, even while important looking nowhere men whisper and click buttons on little matchbox sized phones and touch earpieces like the President of the United States has been threatened, we are treated to a show of magnificent force and procedure, with all seriousness and dedicated melancholy of purpose, when the light skinned black woman who had fought the busty stewardess with the French accent is finally approached and asked to stand up.

She does this in a look of shock and disbelief, as the metal bracelets are clamped down upon her resistance, pulled behind her back without apology, as she is pulled from her upwardly mobile, upper class sophistication into the cesspool of reality. This is the truth that the wrath of man worketh not the righteousness of God, except upon his bloody commissions, when his soldiers are presented the sword of battle. *Put away thy sword,* is the voice she hath heard and denied, to deliver her own version of righteousness at 30,000 feet in the air. And now, as the priced up, prissed out black princess is escorted to the nearest jail cell, she understands that you cannot fight the spirits of God's calling upon those of authority, and you will comply with respect, or you will be made to suffer.

We are kept on this plane for another twenty minutes *after* this woman is taken. It's remarkable to watch and listen to their inability to stay composed, to stay calm and be patient, as the complaining and snappishness grows to a fever pitch in so many people around us, until one woman on the top side of retirement decides she has had enough, standing up and gathering her bags as if she is actually going to be allowed to leave. *Miss, Miss you have to return to your seat*, the stewardess keeps saying, but with no understanding for the older woman's plight, with no concern for her frustration whatsoever, as if the woman were a human carry bag with legs, or some two legged animal with no understanding beyond sentience.

"Miss, you have to return to your seat," is the bitter, passive aggressive refrain, repeated until the captain himself storms out of the cockpit like he's being chased by hounds, threatening the woman with "Miss if you don't return to your seat we will have you arrested. Now please *sit down.*"

"You can't do this to me, I'm an American citizen," are the words that she actually speaks with a straight face, as Anya turns her head towards me and stifles an outright laugh. The woman's humiliation, her embarrassment fills the cold, perfumy air around us with new tension, as she continues to talk and complain through her own degradation and sorrow.

In the aftermath of this tragicomedy in grieving, we are finally given the keys to the gates of Hell, and we exit our snowy plane stage left, walking down the corridor of lost souls to the surprisingly busy main terminal area—Anya in snow bunny white winter coat and scarf, in league with straight blonde hair halfway down the length of her back. I cruise in the wake of her beauty with pride, knowing that every last mother son-of-a-witch of them thinks that she is the prettiest stewardess they have ever seen out of uniform. This Anya Shier, a.k.a. Anya Greenwood is a physical specimen to be admired, to be sure, somehow achieving a radiant glow in her appearance that affects glimpses and stares from at least half of everyone we see, believing that she is some model or covergirl they think they have seen. Ski Slope Barbie she is today, in her thick white scarf, and totally fearless red lipstick and deep blue eye shadow worn in defiance. Anya Aphrodite, she is, possessing an air of confidence in this hoarde of lost humanity that I do not. Though she tells me otherwise, I feel a twinge of ugliness upon myself, bloated and misshapen under my long skirt and coat worn to hide the giant breasts. She believes that I am relaxed but truthfully, my anxiety level is a snowy mountain peak, and my only desire is for us to get away from this beehive of busy bodies going to and from nowhere and back again.

When we finally open the main door, we are reacquainted with the icy realities of an angry Virginia winter, the whole world

beginning to fade into a mist of gray and white, to warn the foolish ones who persist that soon, there will be no flights allowed in or out of this airport. I gladly follow my Anya through the sea of cars waiting, to where our silver SUV is partially frozen in neglect. We make slow and steady work of the fluffy white snow on the windshield and the hood, until the possibilities for our escape finally do appear. Anya gets inside, roaring the engine to life while I glimpse one of the big metal birds lifting away from the snowy ground in a rumbling, thunderous departure.

*Jonathan Lovejoy*

# The Swan Song

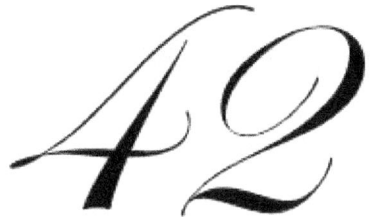

$\mathcal{S}$omewhere in the heart of the city. In the flow of time and history. The statuesque beauty, broad-hipped Brahma bosomed, watches her daughter walk the beam. The daughter of a prosecuting attorney. Mother of a 21 year old gymnast.

The lady lawyer watches her junior in college. Having struggled to balance her studies and her place on the team. Her place of unfulfilled promises. Dreams deferred and dried up from top to bottom. Turned down by every Ivy League and top tier school. Settling for a partial scholarship to State U. To a giant, mega monster sports arena of a learning center. Party school extraordinaire.

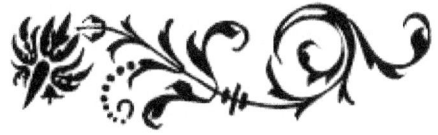

The yellow-pretty gymnast walks the beam. Junior league hippiness unbridled. Secure in her place at the bottom. Lowest scores. Highest point of interest. Practices and meets filled with more lookie-loos than ever. To watch a full blown woman's body wiggle and twist, jump, flip and turn. One of the more physically beautiful, and one of the shapelier gymnasts among them. A princess among the Beccas and the Amandas. Exaggerated breasts and hips excused upon the ethnic body displayed. Full ethnicity displayed in part. Golden yellow skin inherited from the attorney.

In the crowd of clappers. In the sea of smiling silliness. The lady lawyer watches her daughter struggle on the beam. Pulled through the years of her life to this moment. Pulled through by the name Maria Claire. Kimberly Maria Claire. Riding through life upon the Wealthen Stream. Victim of Fate. Having not been granted enough flash and sizzle beyond the face and body to truly impress. In every club. Every organization. Every volunteer this. Every volunteer that. Prime member of every blue ribbon club from kindergarten to college. A weary product of a mother's focus and drive unfulfilled. Vicarious dreams stifled and short. A girl whose victory is in the effort. In the proximity of excellence.

Kimberly Claire walks the beam. Long legs thickened at the top. Hopelessly widened at the hip. A body too conspicuous to ignore. Approached more than once by those who guard the modeling gate. By those who saw her truest life potential. Where her truest gift may

lie in repose. But from fifteen to twenty one, this gate was closed. Locked by Christina.

Christina watches her daughter spin on the beam. Not flinching inside when the girl wobbles. Un-humiliated when she bends all the way forward. Undeterred when she hops to the floor. Un-embarrassed by her climb back up onto the beam, to finish her routine. The place where her life has brought her to. To perform in fear and sorrow in mediocrity. In the burning of blue and black fire.

Pain hidden in full makeup. Secrets in shapeliness borne to infinity. Comfortable in public privacy, that there are none who can suspect the smallest part of what she has known. That there is no scent from the fires in which she has burned. Knowing that there are none who can hear the sounds that echo in her head, from the twilight of recent memory.

Prancing, high stepping, waving her arms gracefully about. Smiling, comfortable in the fine chariot of a life where she is driven. Comfortable that none can see the bruises on her buttocks covered in thick makeup. Bruises explained away as training injuries. Hidden by paint and privilege. Bruises acquired by a mother's rage unleashed in private. By a wooden paddling to her naked skin.

Kimberly Claire is comfortable in the midst of her graceful somersault, that there are none who can feel the pressure. The

pressure upon the back of her neck in her memory, as her mother stands behind her in Full Nelson wrestling hold. Bending her over with her hands locked behind her daughter's neck. Holding her bent over in full strength. Strength superior to her 21 year old daughter's. Strength of mind, body and spirit.

Kimberly walks the beam in comfort. In the comfort of public safety. Behind the curtain of full blown hypocrisy drawn. Content that none can feel the trembling. The trembling that flows through her mother in miniature. The rumbling pre-shocks flowing in waves through her mother's body in private. Pressed so tightly behind her in full standing. Neck already sore from the clamping. From the clamping of her mother's hands locked in.

Kimberly Claire is comfortably hidden by the public ignorance. By their refusal to imagine. Their refusal to believe it is possible.

Christina Claire watches her daughter on the beam. Enamored by her beauty. Comforted by her mediocrity. Confident in her control. Taking a sigh of heavy breasted superiority that none could ever believe. That none could believe in the truth strapped to her daughter. That none could believe in what things were said just this night before. In what vulgarities these depraved orders were given.

Christina looks beyond the daughter's elegant routine. Finding her expression. Feeling the melancholy in her eyes. In the somber, wistful look of relaxed abandon. Understanding that the daughter is in league with her in secret. Knowing that her daughter rests in knowledge, that none can feel what she feels. The broken heartedness. The disillusionment. The inner hopelessness and despair.

Kimberly Claire walks the beam. Burning blue and black fire. Knowing that the fumes of this endtime fire burn unseen. The roaring blaze of her mother's scream in her ears. The look of madness in her mother's eyes still present. The driving into her mother deeply strapped on, on top of her in missionary ad nauseam. Driving downward ad infinitum. Pinning her mother's arms by command obeyed. Slamming into the poor woman until her mind is erased. Until there is no coherent thought possible beyond begging. Beyond pleading for mercy. Hearing her mother's pitiful scream in her ears. Her mother's descent into weeping.

Kimberly Claire walks the beam. Into the high vault elegance of a turning dismount through the air. Her pride and joy. The swan song of her excellent mediocrity. The one claim to superiority beyond her beauty.

Kimberly raises her arms, and flips her head back with her hands as one. Dismounting in old school brilliance. The one exclamation point of her presence. A Kimberly Claire dismount. Elegance displayed in pain.

In beauty.

# The Long
# Road to Oblivion

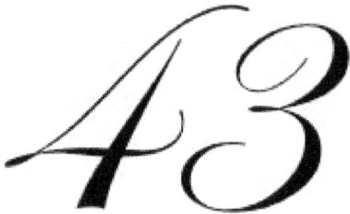

*W*hat is a Breast Queen?

In reality, it is any woman who is obsessed with her own breasts, whether erotic or cosmetic in nature and form. These are the women of any size cup, from the tiny rose bosom to the big boulder bosom, who cannot stop buying bras and cleavage shirts and dresses, who stare at their own breasts like they're watching a movie, or as if they're waiting for one of them to twitch a message that only they can read. These are the women who moan in frustration when their ignorant man is behind them, who take their man's hands and press them to their breasts in squeezing and massaging motion, wishing for a quarter of an hour's worth of what the poor dunce is only going to give a quarter of a minute's time to.

These are the women who try not to yell in victory, when their ignorant man finally puts his mouth to them for more than fifteen seconds of something more than a painful super vac with no technique, who have put themselves to sleep at night with fantasies of their own pathetic man's lips at them in gentle and prolonged nursing. And among these are they which have graduated from the mundane, to leave the natural use of the man far behind, who have allowed the image of their favorite female other, be it from the movie or television screen, to the woman next door in reality.

These are the breast queens, who have allowed their natural concern for their breasts to grow unnatural, to manifest itself in ways both public and private. From the small breasted cutlet cuties, obsessed with their phantom cleavage day in and day out, to the long breasted beauties behind closed doors who understand the pleasures of self-nursing, many of whom know how to do it to their own bodies' devastation and oblivion.

And what is a Breast Goddess?

These are the breast queens who have evolved, many of them prodigies in childhood, who are *deeply* obsessed with their own breasts, *and* the breasts of other women. Their concern is always both cosmetic and erotic in nature and form, but mostly *erotic*— many of them pressed by an inner drive to nude art or photography, or whose obsession has driven them to the far edges of the Lesbian Dynamic and Mystique. These are the moms whose understanding has coalesced, to where the merest touch of their breast is the

invitation to the dance, to the ignition of their body's flame and desire. These are the women who are, ironically, the most covert in public with their attire, but who often do not catch themselves staring intensely at the giant breasted checkout girl in the supermarket, whose big, rounded tits push mightily against their faded pullover shirt, which makes the Breast Goddess feel a twitch in her groin, while she swallows once in her private, mouth-watering obsession.

So many of these are married with children, who have buried this lust deep underneath cultured civility, to where it must be expressed in the unspeakable, to where so many of their daughters have come to know the depth of punishments unmentionable, by way of the belt and the cane upon the front of them. These are those whose self sucking has grown to an art form, where the nursing of their own breasts is as at great length, and is the end result of lust conceived, and the beginning of their bodies' fervent trembling brought forth. The erotic breast obsession of these women knows no bounds, to where interaction with their breasts and the breasts of other women are both the means, and the meaningful end unto itself.

Anya is privy to this, as she lays topless, flat of her back on the sofa in her jeans, while I sit beside her, nude down to my patch of lace black underwear thong and black stockings, leaning over her with my breasts in hand, rubbing the nipple faster and faster against hers while she watches. Enjoying the pitiful anguish on my face, the wrinkled brow in hopeless longing for my body's devastation.

Stopping every so often to satisfy the craving in my mouth, leaning forward to pull one of her nipples deeply upward, letting it bobble free back into place, or raising one of mine up to my own mouth, which so often causes her to say *oh my God* under her breath, with nary an explanation why. But whether she thinks it is bad or good, the essence of beauty or no, it is the drug that lights me up the most at this moment, and I know that it is most likely the final spark to the fuel that has gathered within.

I notice that she says *oh my God* a lot under her breath when we are together, and I am inclined to ask her every so often *"what?"* But I don't need to know this time, whether it is my face or hair, both of which she caresses gently as I am in self nursing repose, both my eyes closed to the world, so that the theater of my mind may burn a light into my brain. This, the light of female perversion; little girls who know the enema nozzle in the daytime dark of their mother's farmhouse, or the lollipop lick of their mother's tongue upon their twelve year old nipples. And this is the source of the moan Anya hears, rather than the pleasure of her hand's gentle caress. It is the taste of the farm girl's young body that I remember, the salty sweet savor of perfection.

Of the long road to oblivion, I can endure no more, and I climb on top of the topless blonde in her jeans, and begin to hop up and down hard and heavy, finding the right rhythm to hammer complacency away, feeling the great breasts slam and slap their message against my body. The sight of me in the black lace underwear string and black stockings, bouncing so heavy atop her transforms her *oh my God* to *oh Dear Lord*, and I open my eyes in time to catch the topless blonde grit her teeth and throw her head back in full resistance to the

energy coursing through her body. But the Force of Destiny will not be denied, and she exclaims in one mighty *yelp* the power of nature, and of what trauma it may produce in the body at will.

And I am suddenly the dominant, slamming hard down upon her without mercy, thrilled to ruin by the pain of unwanted pleasure on her beautiful face, cueing me to take my breast into hand before it is too late, and pull it deeply into my mouth without mercy. I do this, suddenly sparked to a rigid stop, feeling my eyes roll back in my head, while my entire body shakes like a jackhammer at Disneyworld after dark.

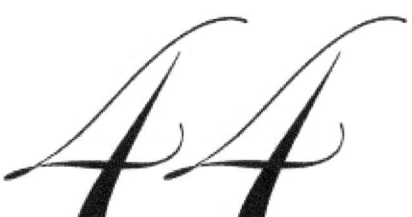

$\mathscr{K}$imberly Claire can feel the spirits ascending. Climbing the stairs in heavy breasted body and form. Middle aged, modern beauty curved to hourglass infinity. Not bothering to knock on the unlocked door of her upper room.

The statuesque, Amazonian woman arrives straight from a day at court. Business suit in plumb prettiness, dark hair to her shoulders in like manner. The woman sits on the bed without words. Staring at the back of her beautiful daughter on her laptop computer, typing away in a fever. Before long, the girl knows to end the pretense. The pretense of cultured civility.

In the spirit of what churns beneath, she rises to her feet, every shapely inch of her taken in by the determined woman's stare. A look of judgment. A somber refrain and reminder.

The girl sits beside her mother. Unable to look up from staring at the floor. Unable to look at the eyes of what portends this part of the timeline. This part of her journey into night.

"What did I tell you would happen," the mother says.

"But I can't control how they score me. I wasn't even the worst one, you saw that."

"All I saw was a little yellow nigger bitch who's too prissy to put in the time and effort to stop embarrassing me at every one of those damn gymnastic meets. *Look* at me, bitch. What did I say would happen?"

The 21 year old daughter can only lower her head. Sniffing once as the tears fall. The mother slides closer to her daughter. Looking at her without touching her.

In the heat of knowledge, where there is no call to pretense, the daughter leans forward and presses her lips hard to the mother's mouth. Of this, the mother owes no resistance, and she responds to her daughter alike in kind. This, until the two women are engaged deeply in a kiss.

In quiet frustration, the mother stands up, and removes her suit jacket in smooth, determined fashion. Exposing the top heaviness of secrets passed down.

"Why are you still sitting there," she says, as the daughter stands up and removes her T shirt and her bra, making quick work of her jeans, breasts hung down low as she bends over. Suddenly feeling

the force of agony slapped into her cheek, causing her to lose her balance and hit the floor in a clumsy heap.

"Did I tell you to take your bra off? Get your ass up and put it back on... you know what, on second thought, get all your damned clothes off and give it here..."

The girl hands her angry mother the bra, then removes the rest of her clothing. Done without hesitation. When she is nude, the mother ties her hands to the front of her body with her own bra.

She stands there in naked humiliation, shapely beyond the reasoning of man. Amazonian curves held in check by the struggle to stay away from the kitchen, and dedication to the brutal gymnastic routine. Rounded breasts still shockingly large for her frame, in disproportionate size and beauty.

The mother removes her business skirt. Unbuttoning and sliding out of her blouse in lavender plumb. Unhooking, slipping away the gigantic bra fabric, sliding her underwear down and away, to reveal the realistic member strapped on. Having been tucked between her legs all day, to remind her of her life's calling. To remind her of what must be.

In heavy breasted, curve waisted repose, hips widened to infinity, she goes to her closet to gather the belt of legend. Walking quickly back to where her daughter stands in waiting. Drawing back to the top of a pendulum swing, whipping the leather down onto the daughter's buttocks with great fire and purpose, until the color of the

girl's skin bears the mark of suffering. Until the girl must cry out from the burning of leather.

The mother retrieves a second flame of fire, from inside the walls of secret. The daughter shakes her head and pleads. But to no avail, as the mother stands behind her again, holding the black caning rod steady. She brings it down in classic *whop* sound through the air, to begin the quick and powerful, the cutting of her daughter's golden yellow skin to blood. The skin of her buttocks is not spared, as is foretold by the renewal of sorrow through her voice, and into the air around them.

And this is done until the daughter's spirit is at the precipice, at the edge of the Forest of Weeping.

The woman grabs her daughter by the hair. Moving her quickly to the corner of the bed. Making her climb onto it on all fours, hands still bound together. Trying to prepare herself for the third part of the truth.

The girl twitches from the spittle. From the stream and droplets fallen in lust from the mother's mouth to her rectum.

Then the room is filled again with sorrow, poured from her voice into their tragic space, as the burning of this flame slides into her bottom from behind. Of what pain of agonizing misery this is, she does not know.

In pleading, she screams her last into bedroom. Into the walls of the upper room. Feeling the heavy breasts come down on her back, as she is held tight without motion. This, until she feels the fire pushed into her again, as the mother's body lurches forward on its own.

Above the melody of her own sorrow she hears the mother exclaim to God, in a mighty yell of agony unleashed. Feeling the woman's body in tension wrapped around her. Jerking forward, as the pain and sorrow passes through.

Jonathan Lovejoy

# Milk and Blood

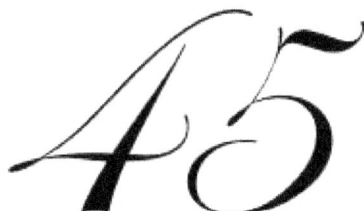

The Kimberly Claire revelation burdens the theater of our minds, being perhaps one of the greatest behind closed doors secrets ever revealed to the world. Anya and I were both held speechless by the NPR lady drone early this morning, who had spoken of a prosecuting attorney from a major (bell) city in Pennsylvania, who was indicted on charges of rape and domestic violence, when a video surfaced after the suicide of her daughter, who was a gymnast at that state's most famous school, a school that had already been burdened with a scandal their legendary football coach carried to his grave after he retired. Anya and I then spent the rare morning in front of the smarmy, aggressively phony morning television W.A.S.P. All *White And So Pretty*, as they reported with teeth gleaming glee the

news of a female prosecutor's arrest and rapid indictment for what was done to her daughter, who posted the video online, where it received 5 million hits before it was finally taken down in its full, unedited form, but to no avail, as it has reappeared in viral form with the nudity in various shades of blur. The girl's laptop computer had been left on behind a screen saver, as she had felt the impending approach of her mother's next sickness, determined to record it for whatever reason, to perhaps show it to her mother in a desperate attempt, in one last plea for mercy. The twenty one year old girl was found by her teenage sister, hanging nude from the upstairs banister, her hands tied behind her back and her ankles bound, suggesting to some that it may not be a suicide at all, and perhaps the lady attorney should be charged with murder. Either way, the suicide note is ubiquitous, in cyberspace for the whole world to see, underneath their smiling picture, *"Because I fucked my mother."*

"I've been having bad nightmares lately," Anya had said before work this morning. "I think I need to stop."

"Stop what?"

"I want us to get a farm," Anya said. "Somewhere like that beautiful prairie green where your mother lives. Maybe she would even let us come live with her for a while. If you could talk her into liking me. I'll never forget the look she gave me the last time we met. If looks could kill."

I had turned the morning news lust down, though not completely off, turning my attention toward whatever plan for her altered destiny she had preconceived.

"We'll raise cows," she said. "Dairy cattle. We'll have all the milk and blood we can drink for the rest of our lives..."

Underneath the Kimberly Claire revelation, I have heard Anya's voice echoing *milk and blood* in my spirit all day, as I have spent the day at the beginning of a new leisure, driving all the way to Washington D.C., to climb the steps of the Lincoln memorial in the snow. The heavy weight of his calling is captured in his features, as I look up into the face of what is surely the Abraham Lincoln Effect, the condition that is pervasive and absolute among humanity, that even as a newborn babe in the backwoods of Kentucky, the shadow of John Wilkes Booth had already loomed over the horizon of his future. Every decision this man made, every decision by the Man of Lean, every decision was part of a series of preordained cause and effect, that ensured he would run for and win his first election for public office in Illinois, and that despite his misgivings to the contrary, every choice made along his path would see him in the halls of the house at Pennsylvania Avenue, where he would dream of having seen his own dead body in a coffin. Every decision made, every little path chosen in care or carelessness would take him to a theater one afternoon, to see a certain play, while the shadow of his future took substance and form in the balcony of the theater, to ring a shot into his head from a pistol, this, from the dark spirit of unseen premonition back in the log cabin, somewhere in the back woods of Kentucky.

On my way back to our palatial property in the Richmond suburbs, the backwoods of Minnesota haunt my spirit in mocking, as though I can see and feel Anya in my heart and mind. Perhaps, she is a country girl at best, tired of the pretense of high class suburban life, where the goal of every single day is to craft and don a false face and clever costume to disguise the truth, to appear to everyone as the perfect projection of perfection. To act as though everyone is perfectly handsome or beautiful, is perfectly healthy, is perfectly wealthy and wise, is perfectly capable of being anyone and anything they want to be, but *chose* not to be President or Empress or Miss Universe because it was somehow beneath them, that they *chose* everything from the hour they split their mother in two being born, to the hour they will split the ground in two at their gravesite. Unable to handle the loss of control that looms, the revelation of Christina and Kimberly Claire, and the answer to the almighty question: "What Churns Beneath Cultured Civility?" As I drive onward in the twilight snow, I am confronted with the reality of latter day secrets uncovered, as acutely aware as any human being ever born the importance of Redemption, to keep my soul from burning forever in the fiery pits of Hell.

An air of mystery creeps around our property in the snow, as I pull into the driveway behind Anya's silver Sonata already parked. Perhaps she is down for one of her many naps, explaining why there are no inside or outside lights on at all. Even so, what explanation

can there possibly be, for the door opened as wide as a movie house entrance, to let in any wayward spirit from their travels in the cold?

Upon this cold and vivid premonition, I move through the door and into the dark'ned house, unable to fight the clutch of evil spirits that dance and walk about me. I pretend not to notice their mocking torment, turning the bright overhead light on to cause them pain, and hopefully send them away. Premonitions are spirits of the future. Either good or bad, hopeful or hopeless, sent back to us as warnings of what things there are to come.

I glimpse at the face of our *Biblis* nude, in her grand repose over the mantle, but receiving no answers from her forthcoming. But somewhere in her frozen expression, in the distant longing, in the profound, indefinable sadness, I can see the edges of a *warning,* and her desire to protect me from whatever darkness there may be looming over this horizon.

All I can do is smile to myself and shake my head, going back outside to the car to gather the bags of nothing gathered in shopping, hauling them back into the house, in grieving to have Anya try on this simple, farmer's wife frock I bought. I want to see the sweetness in her eyes, as she begins to put away the need to be a slave to girl fashion (abandoning it at my encouragement of course), jeans and shirts married to the skin in painted on tightness, those put away for a while, to don the allusion to modesty and feminine humility. And though my blood still burns with these end of the world lusts for perversion, I too understand her sudden need to be free of it—to not be creatures on the dark side of humanity, to no longer emerge from the shadows in death and torment for the innocent. *Milk and blood,* she said, which continues to make me think that it might be better to

leave this suburban pretense behind once and for all, and take hands together by the forests and fields of isolation, under the fading light of the evening day.

Images of my sweet Anya dance and tickle my soul as I climb the stairs, rounding the corner down the hallway to the upper room. Even the lights in the bedroom are off until I click them on, wondering where in the world she can possibly be. *I must have missed her in the kitchen*, is the thought that tries to come up to me in comfort, but is sent away to no avail. And then the truth suddenly rolls in, to fill my soul with a sigh of relief, as I can suddenly see her in the theater of my mind, on the patio outside with a cup of sweet heat in sipping, my Swiss Miss gazing plaintively out over the field of snow, and waiting for me.

An echo of joy and happiness suddenly calls out to me, causing me to smile as I pull the lovely flower dress, the farmer's wife dress I am dying to see her wear. It is a touch of spring in yellow and blue flowers, already married to Anya's blue eyes and golden yellow hair in my imagination. I toss this frock onto the bed, along with my own long winter coat in pewter gray, anxious to get downstairs and out to the patio.

In the dark kitchen, the same spirits of emptiness and abandonment await me as I turn the lights on, unable to push through their barrier of premonition this time, wandering slowly through the empty kitchen, which looks untouched and unmoved by hunger. *Is she really there*, is the question that now haunts my nerves as I get to the patio door, sliding it open to the frigid evening air, staring at the empty patio chairs as if I could somehow will her into existence right in front of me.

I stroll into the icy cold, surveying the great distance of snow covered landscape between the southern mansions, suddenly aware of their status as dens of hidden iniquity. Wondering where in the neighborhood she has wandered to, I turn away from this end of the world arctic cold, strolling back into the kitchen, deciding to check every room in the house before I get into the car and cruise the neighborhood.

As I walk toward the basement door, the portal to our most treasured misdeed, I wonder which of the two teenage girls she may have come in contact with at the neighborhood park, and where in the world she took her in the snow to die. I open the door pointlessly, flipping on the basement light and stepping down the stairs quickly, to check off the first stop on the last search through the house before I begin to panic, and start driving and calling her phone for the rest of the night. I march to the sounds of boots on wooden stairs, down to the concrete basement floor, where the walls are decorated by the invisible screams of the damned.

And when I turn the right corner beside the basement staircase, I am greeted by the manifestation of every tortured screamer held prisoner here, in the pale, lifeless body of the most beautiful blonde woman in the world, lying nude on the basement bed, sprawled naked on her back with lifeless eyes open, and every inch of her white skin covered in bite marks and blood.

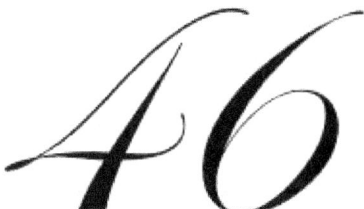

$\mathcal{R}$eal female vampires grow combat claws. They are razor sharp. This is for their ultimate protection when they are attacked, to render a victim as though torn apart by lycanthropy.

At Anya's gravesite, in the crest of new fallen snow, the tips of my fingers are in agony of anticipation, and the tingling in my blood is in grieving for Rage's warm embrace.

Those two bitches are going to die tonight.

Jonathan Lovejoy

# Blackbirds in

# the Snow

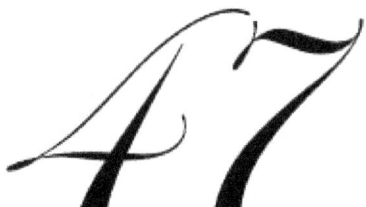

The winter landscape looms heavy over my grief and sorrow, from my place at the gravesite of the one I love, across the open meadow of final resting places, to the snow covered forests and fields beyond. It seems that these are the snowflakes of my every discontent, coalesced from clouds of endtime prophecy and warning.

Oh, what suffering, my dear Anya, did they bring to thine flesh and beauty! How long did they torture and feed upon you my love, before nature took your life from thee! It was the strength of your ancestry, I know, that you could not over power, as they stripped you of your dignity, then cut and tore the life from thee!

Do not torment me, Dear Anya, with the sorrow of the ages, as I see you already in the heart of my soul's memory, held down by the two of them until you were insane with rage and fear—then clawing, biting, and sucking every drop of divine life from thee! Do not make me suffer, dear Anya, when I hear the battle rage in your soul conquered, by two demons more powerful than thee, as you feel the icy touch of death at your feet. Do not torture me in my dreams Anya, when I see the rage in your eyes transfer to fear and sorrow, and I hear you scream my name in the fear of death. Do not haunt my dreams, my dearest Anya, by the writhing of two naked female bodies upon your dying spirit, rendering you helpless unto death in the cold.

What am I going to do now, Anya?

I have nobody.

I have nothing.

I am nothing.

Milk and blood, Dear Anya! Milk tinted as strawberry ice cream, my Darling. Milk tainted as strawberry was your dream. Milk and blood it shall be, dearest Anya. Milk and blood, it shall be.

And now, my love, comes the revelation, the truth of dreams interpreted, as I saw three nights in a row before this very day, two enormous birds of pitch black, walking so casually in the snow of our lawn. But how could I have known that I was being warned? What of the beauty of blackbirds in the snow, in the dreams of dark creatures such as we? Only now, do I understand that those dark angels were not reflections of our sin, but of the tragedy of human existence, which is Fate. They were the demons Death and Hell, this Hell being the corruption of the grave, on this side of eternity. Your spirit cannot rest, Dear Anya, until the promise of God is fulfilled in me—*vengeance is mine saith the Lord, I will repay!*

Somewhere behind these clouds of grieving, I shall take flight again, my Darling, due west toward the Western Gate, to see the sun take upon herself this endtime cloak of amber, to color my flight towards the backwoods of the Minnesota Timberland, where I will deliver the wrath of God to them.

The scent of their misdeed is still strong in my nostrils, dear Anya, illuminating the theater of my mind, as I see you coming down the stairs in hope that there is a package of some sort for you, some snowy winter Christmas come again in commerce wrapped and sent for your pleasure. But I see the terror in your eyes, dear Anya, when you open the door, to see the mature version of your beautiful self, whom you have not seen in more than 10 years—staring at you behind a smile as phony as the ocean is deep, whose head tilts, and eyes twinkle in good natured judgment at you when you speak the

word *"Momma,"* in the pain of bewilderment. A woman who stinks of dirt and the woods, twinged with the grease of oil from the fingers of the lady mechanic she lingered with just a few nights before.

*Momma,* you speak again, as you step outside into the cold, so afraid to invite her across the threshold of our beautiful home, but being unable to resist, as you hear yourself as if outside your own body listening to *"please, come in,"* escorting the mature, voluptuous blue collar queen into your white collar home, sick to your stomach from the scent of sap she brings from the pine woods, and the blood of too many innocent women and children to count.

She is the heavy bottomed version of thee, Dear Anya, the broad hipped side of fifty impending, where her faded jeans display the extraordinariness of womanhood unbridled, and her hoop earrings and perfect white teeth accent the depth of prettiness in the sensuality of Eve. You are afraid, Dear Anya, as the woman hugs you again in the enclosed house, and whispers into your ear the freezing of your blood: *"Your time has come. Accept it, so you won't suffer."*

I can see the terror in your face, my love, as you begin to back away from the heavier, stronger, more voluptuous version of yourself, heeding the warning in your soul to flee, to flee the wrath to

come—for you know already there is no strength in your body to match her power and ferocity, and no strength of resistance to her dominance in your soul.

Flee, my love! Take thine course through the plush, suburban mansion to the back door, to run as far away from this devil as you can get, whom you saw kill your own father when you were but a child of five! Flee through the glass door to the back of your suburban palace, flee to places unknown, and hide until I am there for thee! For I am a foolish woman of leisure now, who will spend her days adrift in travel, and in the relaxed glory of the hunt we live and die to coalesce and to bring.

I cannot be there for you, Dear Anya, as you hurry through to the back of our suburban castle! I cannot be there for you, my darling, when you click the latch on the sliding glass door, and shriek your greatest displeasure to the heavens, when the higher generation of yourself appears like a flash of lightning at the door and walks in, causing you to back into the waiting arms of your mother, where she holds onto you in a grip unlike anything you have felt—until you understand that sometimes in this life, there is no salvation, and no relief from suffering.

Forgive me, my darling! Forgive me for not being there to help thee, in thy desire to run from the two dark spirits from your past, whom you had sworn in private you would never see again— refusing to honor your mother's letters of desperation, the phone calls of hopeless longing unanswered. Forgive me, Anya, because I

was not there when your Russian grandmother (barely aged seven years in her countenance beyond your mother), forgive me for not being there, when she asked you to tell her: *"Where do you take them when you kill them?"*

Forgive me, because I was not there, when you attempted bravery despite your mother's mighty squeezing of the bones in your hand. I was not there, dear Anya, when your mother's mother spoke the words to you: *"You tell me, or I swear I will get the knife and start cutting your fingers off one by one…"*

I was not there, Anya, when the tear streamed down your face in fear and grieving, as you quietly mumbled the words of your secret, forced to speak it louder to her as your mother squeezes you harder at the throat. I am there for your tragic future only, Dear Anya, unable to reach back in the body and give help to thee, when they escort you in the doom of the condemned to execution.

I am not there, Anya, as the older woman begins to disrobe as your mother holds you. I am not there to see the devastation on your face, my love, when you watch a body curved by nature's fiery hand come into view, as naked as the day it was born, firm and fleshy both at once, and curved beyond the reasoning of man, in power exposed;

tight musculature covered in femininity unbridled. Arms thick and heavy with years, breasts hung by the F minor key, a waist both thick and cinched by the inward curve, out into hips spread to vast infinity. Heavy strength, the athleticism of natural endurance carved into the softness of the feminine, to work the magic of living art, and the desire in *"the pit of man's fears, and the summit...of his knowledge."* A body thick with hidden musculature, it is, with breasts drooped in the Armageddon sway, in the way of a Lady Titan, the firm and flopping majesty of a goddess' breasts exposed and forbidden.

I am not there, Dear Anya, as the Lady Titan takes tighter hold of you in your futile struggle, where you know not to unleash your blasphemous rage to them, as your mother removes her golden hoop earrings first, and then every stitch of her clothing to reveal the younger version of the Titan's majesty, the middle manifestation of these three. I am not there, Dear Anya, to see the two naked women rip every strand of cloth from your body, as you begin to plead and cry as a little girl, swearing to please them like never before if they do not hurt you, if they will allow you to return to a normal life of hope.

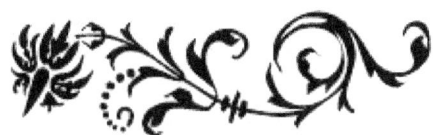

Forgive me, my darling, for not being there, when your mother was laid underneath you, as her mother was laid on top of thee, to

where they could feel you sandwiched between them, as you began to scream from the fear of panic and premonition joined as one, as their grips around you become filled with unholy scratchings upon your skin, and your mother allows herself a classic hiss of warning, that the Lady Titan may begin to nourish her soul with the fear that pours from thee. Please, do not try to fight them, my dearest Anya, do not fight the irresistible force and the immovable object that has come for thee. Close your eyes, Baby, that you may not see the most fearful sight in all of latter day womanhood, when the eyes of your ancestry glow as white as marble, and the sharp pointed death begins to gleam at the taking

of your soul to Hell.

By the hand of God, dear Anya. In the fires of your screams. There is forged the Sword of Battle, which is bestowed to me this day, my Love. In this hour, on the eve of fire and brimstone from Heaven.

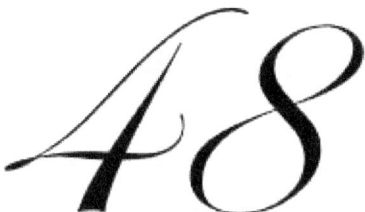

These are the stars of a moonless night, sent to comfort me in my flight. Gaze upon my peril, O Lord—cherish me in my fight.

I walk the streets of this Minnesota town. Somewhere nearby the Northern Wood. Thankful that the gray skies have parted this brief path I walk, in the dark of this fervent night. I have disembarked my rolling chariot, after my flight from the snowy east, walking the last mile in the isolation and the cold. Seeing only the darkened silhouette of these north woods under cloak of night, underneath the infinity of stars in the heavens.

The earth underneath my feet crunches, under the thick coating of white fallen from winter skies. Given this brief reprieve nearby the end of my plight. This, despite what odds there may be against me, the stars do beckon as a sign unto me, that I have divine approval for this pain, and what expression there is of it there must be.

I turn right at the mailbox alone on this country highway, walking down the long road into the Minnesota woods, already seeing the faint glow of life in the cabin in the clearing of the wood. There is nothing of me but my stretchy pants in black, with shoes built for movement in battle, and the sporting top to hold the mountainous flesh into place. I walk this road in the agony of the cold, in the pain of this nighttime renewal, ready to do battle with the forces of what is meant to be, and what dark angels and demons there are that lie in wait.

A flash of what golden haired, blue eyed love that I have lost sparks a streak of red hurt through my chest to the pit of my soul, to remind me that there is no mercy inside the gates of Hell, and that they have abandoned hope, when they choose to enter in thereat. The determination of the fiery pit burns through the paling blue of my eyes, and the mind of Eve colors the length of my darkened hair at midnight.

I walk boldly up the steps of isolation, to the door of this out of the way place. Told by the spirits of what must be to slam both fists upon it, to rise them both from the stupor of backwoods complacency, and to prepare myself for the impending crashing in.

The pain of my heart feeds this determination, and even as I hear the brave, feminine voice cry out in vulgarity, *"who the fuck is that!"* I have decided that this is the first of three final blows to the stability of this backwoods door. And upon the second blow, I feel the tearing of wood, as the steel of what hopelessly inhabits space as a lock pulls against the very frame of the door. And I draw upon the strength of my lost love, the power of my hopeless future, and I roar as an animal brought forth from the netherworld, crashing the wooden door away from its sad state as locked—pushing it open into the world of the condemned woman, and her mother of strength and power forlorn.

With nary a hesitation, with nary a spoken word in the nighttime cabin, I run in unseen ability of motion, toward the sensual woman in white t-shirt and blue denim shorts, digging my claws into her shoulder and her breast, sinking my teeth into the white of her lovely neck, unaffected by the strength and power of ferocity that I feel from her, with a greater determination of will than what is humanly possible upon her skin, until I am aware of the taste of her blood, even while I feel the tearing of her claws in my arm, and at the skin of my back. This, while I must suddenly endure the heat of a stinging bite upon the very middle of my back, which causes me to have to let go of my first victim, and turn my attention to the bigger, stronger devil upon my back...

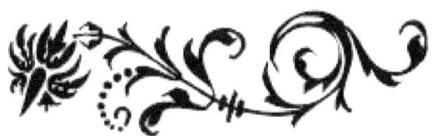

I turn and grab her face with both my hands, a face twisted in unfathomable rage, flipping over on top of her in strength that

exceeds her own, and in the lust to taste the poison of her tainted blood, and to swallow it to quench a thirst unlike any I have ever known. In the swiftness of instinct, I slash my hand across her face in tragic accuracy, to ruin what perfect beauty was there, and to mark the place where I must sink my teeth in uncompromising fury. This, I do with no hesitation, overpowering her to brief fear and agony, as she screams her daughter's name in dreadful form, so that I may hear the distinguished mark of Fear of Death in her soul.

And from this bite fully engaged upon her face, I move to the white skin of this Lady Titan's neck, and I hold on for dear life, biting all the way through, tearing away, then biting another part of her neck in the ferocity of a lady grizzly doused with acid, until I can feel nothing of her daughter's pathetic attempt to bite into me, or to claw me away from her mother's certain death.

Of this, I hold on to sufficiently, until she is weakened just enough, flipping myself to her daughter and grabbing her tight, burying my claws into her face, ripping the cloth of her shirt with the skin of her breast underneath, holding her by the throat, biting full into her breast to taste the blood through them, then to return to the feast of her neck already torn to red bone flesh and blood.

I lay down upon this beautiful woman in the heat of unfathomable rage unbridled, drinking the sweet life from her as she struggles underneath me, the woman trembling and shaking in unholy spasms to stay awake, as I feel the hot blood pumping into my mouth, encouraging me to drink my fill until the pumping has ceased to be. Upon this mother's daughter I rest, feeling myself return to sanity, as if lowered to safety from the deadly heights of a treacherous mountain to the nighttime valley forest below. I hold on to this woman until she does not move, until the tension in her muscles gives way, and I cannot feel the beating of her heart in my body. I hold on in a stupor, drunk with the blood of this murderess, holding on until I see her mother leap towards me again, whereupon I flip her over in bloodlust renewed, to clamp upon the bloody place torn already from her neck, to drink the poisoned blood of the ancestry, to feel the last of her titan's strength fade from her muscles, until I feel the departure of her condemned soul from her body.

And up, upward from my bloody repose I climb to my feet, arms and back on fire from the bites and scratches of battle, to the kitchen of these like women, knowing that the sharpness of meat cutting steel must lie in wait, to keep the lust for animal flesh fed from the cutting board to the dinner table. Of this, I see unsheathed as if in waiting, the butcher's blade from a rack of beef ribs done in craving, taking the blade to the living room in absolute bravery, to start with the neck of the lady titan, and of what happens to the head attached, when the sharpness of a butcher's blade is thrust upon it.

# 49

A real vampire is the devil in disguise

With naught but loveliness in her eyes

To hide the mountain of her soul's deceit

'Til your flesh and blood are become hers to eat

# Iris Greenwood Rides the Wind

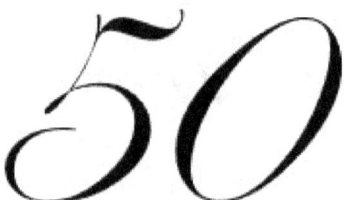

*I*ris Greenwood rides the wind. The winds of sanity come and gone. Having lured and killed the female prison guard she befriended, the one whose trust she had gathered and secured. This, four months ago, in the heart of the summer season. But now, in the chill of the autumn outside her window, she rests weary at the edge of another attack, where the straight jacket will be justified. To prevent the clawing and biting of the attendants in the asylum. In the place for the criminally insane.

She rests in her chair. Her arms bound to her sides by the cloth of shackles and latches, insuring that she can be overcome by them. When they attend to the process of her subjugation. The process of her dismantling. The slow, steady removal of her humanity.

Iris Greenwood rides the wind. On the edge of roaring madness unleashed, where the sharpness of her teeth will be soundly dismissed. Where the whiteness of her eyes will be dealt with in epic hypocrisy. Where the report of the animal clawing to death of a female prison guard will live on in legend only. Reduced to "exaggeration" on paper. Prison officials "embellishing" a troubled case, that they might be rid of her once and for all. There are no monsters in real life, they say. Only minds and motivations of the sick, the twisted, and the damned. There are no ghosts. No werewolves. No vampires.

Iris Greenwood rides the wind. At the edge of a craving instinct. Where she can take in no other food but human flesh. No drink other than human blood. She rests at the edge of a last mile through the wilderness of this life. Where the curse of Death will finally begin to have its way. Where the beauty that gave rise to the myth of their immortality will be tainted. Where the youth and beauty of her body will be corrupted. Until the stresses of her new calling will take over her mind and her features, until the transformation to the purity of her blood will be complete.

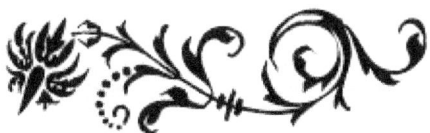

In the cold breezes of a November wind. On the eve of winter's call to oblivion. She waits for the arrival of them again. That she may deliver her last burst of speed and strength reborn. This, as she

begins to feel the fabric of her restraint begin to give. As the tearing of the shackling cloth has begun. Knowing that before the end of her days, before they bury her alive, she must have one last feeding to bear. The death of the middle aged nurse. The one who judges. The one who patronizes. The one who revels in the agony of her electric shock therapy. Who delights in listening to her yelp in agony when the fire starts.

Iris Greenwood rides the wind. At the edge of her last freedom. The edge of her last feeding. The last cutting of innocent white skin to blood.

The tearing of the shackle cloth thrills her to the bone. Freeing her arms for what must be done. For the exclamation point that must end her life. To perform the secret depravity, buried from the eyes of a dying generation. From the lying eyes of a people lost in ignorance. A people at the edge of Judgment. At the edge of an apocalypse. The burning of blue and black fire.

Iris Greenwood rides the wind.

On the eve of eschatology.

# The Daughters of Eve

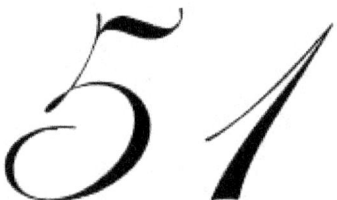

$\mathscr{I}$languish in the middle of the snow covered open prairie, a prisoner of the woman who gave me life, and took it from me so abundantly. I am burdened by the memories of motherhood gone awry; a woman whose orgasms come in threes, and are truly devastating to her mind and body. I am but a single day's removed from the end of my journey west, where I sought the heads of the two Gorgon Medusas, at the edge of the northern Minnesota wood. Under the cloak of a starry night, I was the image of battle worn fury unleashed, walking the snowy nighttime road, carrying a woman's head in each hand, determined to have their lifeless eyes gaze upon the nighttime once more as I walked, to remind them of the life that once was, before drifting into eternal earth sleep, and opening their eyes in the fiery pits of Hell.

Nearby my rolling chariot of death, I drop the two bizarre flowers plucked from their stems in fatal beauty, hearing their muffled thud upon the cushion crusted layer of ice and snow at my feet. Soon, the two of them are as individually wrapped as yellow rose flowers sent to a life going nowhere, placed in black plastic in the trunk, for the two day's leisure journey east, where I buried the poisoned corrupted petals of gold stained with blood in the woods behind our palatial, suburban property. It was a drive I surely had to make coming back. Oh, what an amusing time it would have been, to have seen their smiling, skeletal faces on the airport x-ray machine, gliding in their bags from one side of Security's bewilderment to the other!

From the tragicomedy of their laughing skulls, I am pulled away to this part of the timeline, but one turning of the day beyond the threshold. This, the threshold of a life I had fought for so many years to escape, learning that Predestiny is as the whirling vacuum of a funnel cloud. I knew this, when I saw the body of my Anya in naked, bloody repose in the lower room. I knew this, when I stood beside the black marble gravestone, and placed the white rose flower upon it in memoriam. I knew this, as I crashed the cabin door, at the edge of the Minnesota Wood. I knew this, as I buried the heads of the Killing Bitches in the suburban Virginia Wood. I knew this, as I was drawn by this funnel cloud to the open Virginia farmlands, to the door of Elizabeth Greenwood. I knew this, when Betty Greenwood opened the door, and I gazed upon the eyes of Creation passed down, through the seven millennia of East of Eden. I knew this, when I pushed my way to an icy hug, where the statuesque, voluptuous beauty only went through the motions of compassion, as I began to sob in her arms. I knew this, when she escorted me on the edge of

hysterics to her comfort cushioned sofa and sat beside me, as I laid my head upon her bosom and wept.

Of Predestiny's power and pull, I know this, as I stand at the precipice of the evening day, thankful for the grieving sky's brief respite from sorrow, and the beauty of the deep twilight, nearby the edge of night. I know this, as I look upon the fervent glory of the passing comet, wondering of what dark future it portends, or if it is indeed a harbinger of nothing. Above the winter comet that dives toward the Western Gate, I am mocked by the essence of true beauty, by the Moon waxed right into a crescent sliver, in companion with the star that rules the coming night. Of Predestiny, I know this, as my soul drifts across the snowy field to the two story, white country house all aglow, where one of the daughters of Eve prepares for us a cooking feast inside. Of this, I already know, that I will torment this woman in whispers, until she lets me nurse at her bosom. And at last, of this I know, that as surely as I stand in the twilight snow, beneath the emerging stars of heaven, that among the types of fear this woman will soon distinguish, will be the fear of being raped by her daughter.

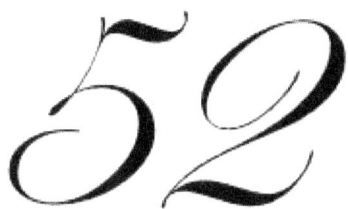

My mother's hypocrisy knows no bounds, in the shadows of the evening day. Even at the dinner, my groin aches with memory, in the snowstorm of her pious judgmentalism, as I remember her stark naked and hop-frogged on top of me when I was but a child of thirteen. Having discovered the early appearance of my anomaly that skipped her generation, the clitoris capable of such growth as to be unfathomable. Even at thirteen, it was large enough to be pronounced when I was aroused, which delighted her to no end, causing her one day to lay me naked upon my back, pulling my young nipples into her mouth until she watched it grow like a sprout from a seed, all pink and perfectly rigid, and so sensitive to the touch as to be painful under too much pressure.

At the dinner table of her pretense, my mind is ablaze with the image of this beautiful, giant breasted woman with her legs spread wide, squatted down over me in leap frog position, first grinding against it in staring madness, staring down at it as she rubbed it against hers in a grinding squat, in a squatting grind of pure writhing abandon, and then slamming herself up and down upon it like she was trying the break the bed through my body. The memory of her long, heavy breasts flopping as she bounced still slaps a rhythm in my ears a score of years later, where I can see the first shock of lightning pass through her body, to make her stop bouncing and start trembling from head to toe, her mouth hanging open, eyes unable to focus as the first wave passes through. And then she falls to her knees from her squatting position, as her body starts to shake again, grabbing onto the bed linen for a reprieve that can never be. Regretting that she unleashed this raven into herself, looking at me for help that I cannot give her past a hard, twisting pull of her great nipples, as she begins a third ride, this time unable to keep a brief siren from escaping her voice. She cums in triplet, this breast goddess among women, she spasms the rippling of an earthquake times three.

Whether or not this is completely unique among women, I do not know. I do know that the memories of how long I have held her from behind through her trembling have begun to haunt me since I arrived,

made more intense by her pretense, this latter day chastity she hides herself in.

"What's wrong with a daughter nursing at her mother's breasts in private?" I say.

"Because it's *incest,*" she says, in full, southern church gothic, gigantomastia bound up in a bra so big and tight that every inch of her breast mountains are covered under her dress, and she can hardly draw a deep breath without putting some effort into it.

"What I did with you when you were growing up, I'm sorry. All I was doing was mimicking the behavior I experienced from your grandmother."

"And you didn't enjoy it?"

"I didn't say that. We always enjoy the pleasures of sin for a season. And then, we reap the consequences of what we sow."

And what consequences are these, Mother? Is it the pain of orgasms so severe, that they leave you spent and weeping?

"Why are you so afraid to be who you are?"

"Like your grandmother was? Maybe you haven't been caught yet, Iris. But I know what you are. You and that girl you just buried. Like I said... you reap what you sow."

"Well, if that's true... then you still have some reaping to do, don't you Mother?"

"Don't you threaten me," she says. Staring at me in somber faced piety. "I won't be dragged down to the pits of Hell by the likes of you. If you're going to stay here, you will respect my decision to turn away from who I was then."

"Respect your decision to deny yourself? To pretend you're not still boiling in the same end of the world lust that you pulled me into when I was just a child?"

"You shut your mouth."

"I will *not.*"

"Not another word about it or I will throw you out of this *house!*"

The force of her anger betrays her desperation. The years of battle frustration built up, trying so hard to pray and preach herself clean, by sheer force of will to keep her thoughts and sensibilities bound up as tightly as what her undergarment has hidden beyond my sight.

"I will leave when I am good and ready. And I have earned the right to say whatever the *Hell* I want. To say whatever the *fuck* I want."

"Don't get too comfortable then. Because one way or another, I will be rid of you."

"Listen to yourself," I say. Unable to stop the mist from forming, gathering and streaming once down my cheek in front of her. "How do you think that makes me feel? You care more about your precious Bible and trying to hide like some fucking *vampire* now than you care about your own daughter."

"Interesting word you chose," she says. Tickled inside to a delight that shows through the anger on her face. "Vampire."

The truth in quiet, triumphant accusation raises me quietly, regrettably from my hungry place at the table. Turning away respectfully in one last pathetic sniffing, walking from the kitchen to the bottom of the living room stairs. Taking each step in greater pain than the last, drifting past the portrait of Bouguereau's *Little Thief*

staring at me in mocking, on my way to a sleep of grief and sorrow in the upper room.

Jonathan Lovejoy

# The Rape

## of Iris

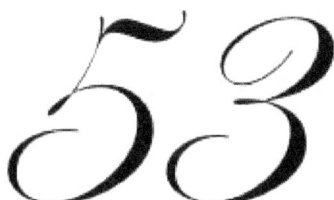

The weeks pass into oblivion, until I am at one with this waking nightmare, tormenting me  day and night with images of me laid strong and fast on top of my mother, both of us stark naked, with me holding her down as she screams in helpless abandon. I have awakened from the torment of this dream one time too many, gliding down the stairs in full battle gear, which is only a certain plain, flower made country dress, of the kind worn when feminine comfort is key. In the kitchen, mother is already in her casual, going to meeting attire as if she had a library cart to push, gigantic bosoms nicely hidden in the navy blue dress cloth buttoned up to the neck in determination.

I wander casually in, the Italian Girl in Algiers, which is but a brunette nothing in tragic lack of fashion, content that no other human being but my mother will ever see me in this country house attire.

I speak my good morning to her while she is at the stove, preparing to satisfy our vulgar appetites with the bacon and eggs of legend, stepping boldly up behind her and kissing her on the cheek too long, which causes her to turn to me in *fungalooga* and say brilliantly: "You're in a good mood this morning," turning back to the sharp knife, and the slicing of the pack of bacon through. "But shouldn't you be wearing a bra," she says. "You know how inappropriate it—"

And the words are cut off by my lips pressed at her cheek again from behind, causing her to turn and look at me in full, motherly disapproval—which only serves up a deeper beauty in her shocked, somber expression…

"What are you *doing,"* are the words that she cannot hold back, as I reach down to gently place my hand at the knife, lifting it from her hands and placing it onto the stove.

"I want you to *stop,"* she says, refusing to turn away from the stove to me, as I grip her tighter from behind, staring directly at this beauty in country sophistication, her hair pinned up and ready for battle against her raging blood's depravity.

"I told you this was *not* going to happen," she says, picking up the knife again, of which I am fully prepared, squeezing her wrist just enough to bring a suffering to the edges of her expression.

"Put it down."

But her stubbornness brings a harder squeeze at her wrists, of which she is determined to fight through, until the words slip out, "You're hurting my *wrist."*

"I said put it *down."*

And the squeeze upon her wrists this time is enough to remind her of the truth, of the reality of this end of the world dynamic, and she drops it noisily, frustratedly onto the stove.

"Please, stop," she says, in a deep, breathy desperation, as my lips return to the side of her face again, turning her face to mine in a futile attempt to speak, but instead meeting me mouth to mouth— with me pushing harder against her, causing her to grunt deeply in the locked kiss, a grunt of helpless desperation, unable to stop the sudden ignition of a flame long since suppressed and snuffed out in her body through will power alone. But the feel of my lips at hers, the probe of my tongue, the taste of it in her mouth causes her to wander at the edges of reason, in fear of what traumas are in store for her mind and spirit.

Instantaneously, I hear the fire in her breathing, and feel the desperation of resistance growing in her body. She releases my tongue in a long, kissing pull, with me still behind her, begging me once more "please don't do this to me," as I spin her around and press her against the kitchen counter, pressing my lips and tongue to her beautiful neck in a deep sucking, which I know causes her eyes to roll back as she tries to gather herself in strength against me, succeeding in putting her arms between us and trying to push and fight me away, even managing to push my face, which only excites a more aggressive spirit, making me lift her up in the ease of what strength I possess, carrying her bodily across the kitchen into the livingroom, slamming us down full bodied onto the plush, comfort cushioned sofa.

On top of her, I watch her work herself into a frenzy of false chastity, into a frenzy of moral hypocrisy, into a delusion of judgment and morality.

"I told you to *stop* it," she says, teeth clenched, beautiful features twisted in anger, as she makes a valiant attempt at full resistance, fighting and pushing against me until I have had enough of it, and I grab both her wrists, slamming them back hard onto the sofa, pinning them beside her head. From this position, I rest my heavy breasted self to her, letting her arms go while I lay tightly against her, pulling her dress up past the black silk stockings, exposing her thighs to the cold of the daytime dark around us.

The types of fear are many, and uniquely distinguished. Among these is the Fear of Rape. Which begins to take hold, transforming the anger in her body into a ghostly mist of pure terror.

"Please don't do it," she says, "I don't want it to happen to my body. I don't want to let them in. They'll take over me again if I let it happen..."

And what vain babblings are these, dear Mother! I choose not to know, as I pull my dress up, to place myself to her front to front, which causes her to cry out "no" once very loudly, staring off in madness to a brief distance, as though she can see the approach of something unearthly, and unendurable to her mind and body.

But the scream only reaches out to my hips to raise them high and involuntary, slamming them back down to her groin as hard as I can, a feeling which spreads her legs apart just enough, causing her to grab onto me for dear life as I slam into her hard again, holding myself there on top of her, clamping my lips to her neck again in deep sucking, listening to her scream for mercy at the top of her lungs: "Please *STOP!*" Which only serves to connect me to her fear of this unwanted devastation, causing the inevitable motion to take over my hips, and I slam into her repeatedly as she screams in angry fear, until her voice is joined by mine, and the wailing of a siren call into the morning air.

The wailing cry of my voice has its undesired effect of her, and she must grab onto my dress at my hips, to push herself upward in a rage of desire, until her screams of fear and rage are transferred into long, weeping cries of hopelessness and sorrow, as the suppressed energy explodes into her body, causing a haze in her vision, as both her legs begin to spasm, amidst the cries for mercy and forgiveness into the walls of her isolated country home.

Jonathan Lovejoy

# The Call of the Motheress

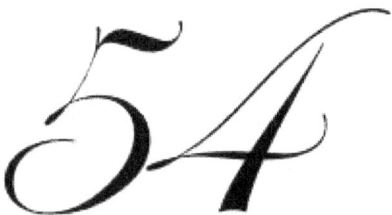

The walls of hypocrisy have fallen like Jericho, leaving the pain of truth and beauty in its wake. What definitions of lust, sin and depravity there are have clawed their way back into our lives through the walls of secret, leaving the two of us as victims of screaming devastation and ruin. Every inch of this woman, I have tasted. From the bottom of her feet to the highest patch of skin at the top of her forehead, when her hair is pulled back and pinned tight so as not to get in our way, this, with the hair of her daughter in full brunette mane, that she may gaze upon the wilderness of my allure in fascination, and an end of the world lust and desire in the aftermath

of such trauma—I am often atop of her sprawled nude upon her back, having held her pinned in one way or another as she endures the explosions in her body, listening to her grieve and beg the Almighty for mercy that will not be given, begging me for compassion that will surely never come.

I will be atop this goddess in my own exhaustion, lollipopping her from her breasts to her shoulders, from her neck to her chin, from her chin to her lips, from her lips to her nose, from her nose to her cheeks, from her cheeks to her eyes, then going back to dry every cold and wet place I have created on her skin with kisses, stopping at her neck again to give deep kisses and suckings to light and heavy bruises, understanding that in the history of my life, the sweat of another hath never tasted so sweet, nor hath the tiniest drop of blood pricked from another's skin rang the chimes in my body such as hers. Even the blood of a young girl, even the screams, even the smell of fear from their innocence cannot replace the Call of the Motheress, which is for a daughter to partake of the sensual pleasures of her mother's mind and body.

In the aftermath of this grieving, I am often laid atop her in full dominance, pulling a single breast of hers up into my mouth in

repeated shaking, releasing it in the loud, popping suck over and over, my eyes rolling back at times in disbelief at what manner of pleasure it is to have her breast in my mouth, with her pinned underneath me in the aftermath of trauma. And this I have done far beyond the quarter of an hour, until I have heard her breathing return to its state beyond control, and in a quiet moan that flows through her as from beneath the earth, her body will begin to shake of its own accord underneath me, as she achieves the Witch's Crown by way of the Nun's Intercourse, which is the nursing of the breasts to full completion.

It hearkens back to her original calling as a breast goddess, which was made known to me in my youth, when my little thirteen year old hands would struggle to hold the heavy things up, with her nipples pulled deeply in my naïve little mouth. I would wobble and release, suck, wobble and release this breast to her continued devastation, feeling the lightning strike me hard enough to make my body twitch just once, as she lay underneath me in renewed suffering. Then at long last, my last bobble of bubble gum bosom is come and gone, and I allow my tongue to take me where it will to her body, either north to her fervent and most cherished release in a kiss, or south, to where her begging is renewed to eventual screaming again, and the return of the Armageddon Quake to every bone and muscle in her body.

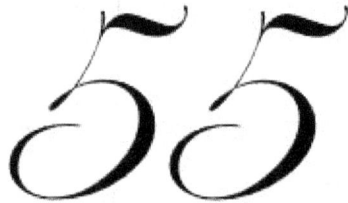

"*Let's go home so I can fuck you in the ass…*"

These were the words I whispered in vulgarity to her in church this very hour, standing up in the middle of the preacher's droning— dry dragging us through blood and fire and vapour of smoke— whispering it loudly and directly into my mother's ear, then standing up and walking out of the sermon with the rest of the deaf ears, none of them having the strength to break away from their dead eyed Lutheran stupor and walk out themselves for the last time. I only went out of deference to my mother's curse, which is to be a slave to church attendance once a month, believing it may actually contribute

to saving her from the coming judgment of fire and brimstone upon the earth. I had walked in the lobby not more than thirty seconds before she was behind me, lips tucked in prim and proper in full wintry church attire, barely able to look me in the eye as we walk the snowy distance to the car. But I boldly take my mother's arm, reaching up to kiss her on the cheek as we walk, if for no other reason than to scare the devil out of her that one of her churchified acquaintances might suspect that she is fucking her own daughter in private.

We barely cross the threshold of the white, country house before I have her pressed up against the wall to taste her powdered peppermint breath, and to breathe in the essence of her shampoo and light perfume. I decide to delight in the squeal of fear and shock by lifting her off her feet in perfect ease, carrying her over my shoulder like a busty sack of grain, hauling her up the stairs to hear her beg me to please stop, while she rides up the stairs upon her strong daughter's shoulders, genuinely afraid that she might fall and break her neck. But the strength of the ages is in every muscle and bone, as I haul this Amazon all the way to her bedroom, tossing her to the bed, and watching her helplessly try to recover her lost church dignity.

"Take off all your clothes," she says, voice trembling. "So that you can do to me what you promised."

This, I do. When I am disrobed, this woman fully dressed in heels, skirt and blouse, grabbing both my breasts and attacking the

nipples one by one, her church dignity flowing out into the air around us in a gruff, bellowing grunt of lust and desire.

"Take off *my* clothes," she says, "so I can feel your girl cock in my ass."

This, I do. Restraining myself from the ripping, the tearing of her blouse to shreds as I unbutton it just enough to pull it over her head. The tight, deep charcoal skirt is next, sliding it down and away from her black, bikini cut underwear and black lace stockings, all framing a set of hips too fearfully curved and fully packed to look upon. I slide the underwear cloth down and away,then making quick, unceremonious work of the lovely black stockings, after her black heels are kicked off to the side and forgotten.

"No, leave my bra on," she says. "I don't deserve to have them touched. I am a filthy, whoring excuse of a woman, and I need to be punished for it."

She escorts me to the edge of the bed, where I sit, looking up at her in awe, feeling the spirit of rare lust being conceived in her, to bring forth the sin of this new devastation in her upper room. She turns her big backside to me, which is truly remarkable to behold,

given space to rule the court of curviness by the imprisoning of her breasts in the big, black bra above.

"Spread my ass open," she says. "*Wider.* Now, spit in my ass… yes, let a big glob of your spit fall on my ass, so you can put your finger in it. Can you do that for me? Can you put your finger in my ass?"

After the spit from my mouth has fallen, I slowly push my middle finger into her rectum, amazed at the strength and power flowing from her voice, sounding as if she were enduring the agony of something four times thicker than a finger.

"Yes, push it in… push your finger in your mother's sinful ass… *YES!!*"

And upon this last, loud syllable is my own awakening, feeling the need to stand up and embrace her from behind.

"Are you going to do it to me now," she says, her legs trembling as I press myself against her. "Are you going to fuck me in my ass like you promised?"

"Yes."

"Yes, what?"

"Yes, Mother."

"Open me up again," she says. "I need to feel your wet girl cock in my ass. Put it in for me…"

This, I do. Sliding the first of a full six inches of pure, skin-on clit up into her bottom, causing her to scream an angry, warrior woman's yell as before, which pulls a wave of energy from somewhere in my own groin and backside, causing my body to lurch forward against her on its own.

"Don't move," she says. "Please don't move again, don't make me cum yet... let me feel your girl cock deep up inside me before I cum."

But this prim, proper woman's behind closed doors behavior has gripped me without mercy, and even without moving another inch, the siren call grown inside finds its way into my voice and loudly into the bedroom. It was a valiant, concerted effort on my part to remain still and silent, but to no avail.

The sound I make, and the twitching of my body prove too much for her own resolve, and remarkably, with nary a sound, I watch her legs and buttocks begin to quiver with the force of a washing machine gone haywire. This trembling goes to the rest of her, as she reaches back to take my hand, holding on as the wave returns again, punishing her this time enough to bring a soprano shriek, then a lesser shriek, as the quivering returns a third time passing through.

"*I*'m going to have to fuck you."

And this, I say with near apology, when the lust in my heart has grown beyond my girl cock's prowess to express, having to don that which pertaineth to a man, strapped in realism about my hips, hung down big and long, as the fullest expression of what I must do to her in this church hour come and gone.

I stand above her, with her on her knees before me, still half spent from what had come but a few moments before. Sliding all of the

eight inch sword to the back of her willing throat and beyond, looking up at me in pleading to be allowed to breathe, but with no mercy from me, grabbing the back of her head and holding her there, shaking my head, *no*, Mother. You will not be allowed this brief respite, before you are hit by the truth, the truth that gags from deep within, making you cough as my hips twitch in response, finally allowing you to pull the long lady cock out of your mouth, watching the spit fall to your breasts, as the tears roll down your face in the choking cry. I watch you be taken over by this fever, grabbing onto it with the strength of your hand in the stroking, putting your mouth upon it again, sliding it deep into your throat in defiance to me, choking upon it again, while I hold your hair in place, saying *"no, don't you take it out of your mouth, keep it down there, keep it there so I can cum."* And I watch you suffer this end of the world gagging, Mother, until my hips twitch with warning again, letting you pull away in the spitting choke, the gagging of your own lust in spittle from your mouth down to your breast again.

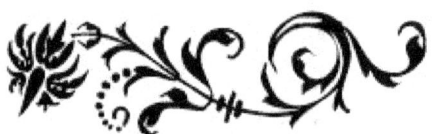

I stand you up to your feet before the mirror of our upper room, the reflection of our misdeed, turning you in gigantomastia exposed and hung down, watching the mirror capture your breasts in swinging repose, the moving picture of Olympian breast beauty in the world. Behind you, I take the member hung down into my hand, placing it at the center of life, the origin of all life, pushing the head of it into you from behind, watching your face twist in the shock of

this revelation, the fullness of Estros touched by Testros, sliding so big into your proper place from behind, watching your Amazonian strength be conquered by the lady cock, the great member of truth and legend, which must conquer your femininity for a time, to bring you under my perfect will and desire.

From the big cock slid halfway into her, I slam it home without warning to her womb, making her flinch and yelp in pain, and the lightning flash of a pleasure that she only thought she understood. With myself tucked away deep inside her, I lean over her back heavy and strong, gathering myself nearby her beautiful ear, to breathe my heavy hearted warning to her once again, *"I'm going to have to fuck you,"* to which she responds by nodding her head in full surrender, and the understanding of Eve passed down.

I stand up straight, slamming into her again hard once more, to see her great body jerk, and to hear her beautiful voice yelp its displeasure, holding her by her curved waist tightly, and beginning to slam this endtime message home to her that no, this time there will be no salvation, and no deliverance from suffering. Far beyond my need for my body's shaking, I know that my pleasure will be her pain—this, the pain of her body's shaking times three. And though she pleads for genuine mercy, to be released from the pain of what she cannot endure, from a pleasure divined from places otherworldly, and bestowed unto her—though she begs me for a reprieve, I know that there can be none given, until I achieve the soprano
shriek from her.

In the spirit of what strength and sadism I can achieve, I begin such a rabbit rhythm into her as to be unfathomable, until almost immediately, the high pitched song from her voice begins, singing her ruin to the rafters, to the roof of our country house and beyond.

But no, dear Mother, there will be no mercy—no checkpoint for you to catch a breath, as I continue this rapid, unflinching drive into her from behind, to remind her that she is still a woman, and that this is the fullness of what instrument that Nature hath designed her to be. The room around us is alive with her screams, while the second wall of her resistance falls in the midst of them, carried along on the current of high pitched yelping without ceasing, to where what shaking there is in her body is as much from my pounding from without, as from her body's pounding back to me from within.

In the spirit of the masculine channeled through the feminine, I lay into her with the purpose of killing her resolve, killing her strength of womanhood, breaking her down before me to nothing. And in keeping with the prowess of our union this day, I hear the last

of her song in triplet escape through her yelping shrieks, giving my soul permission to take hold of me at my hips and groin, to cause me to yell the angry warrior's cry of battlefield victory, as I must slump over the back of this condemned woman in full exhaustion, feeling her body's lurching and the remainder of these end of the world spasms passing through.

Jonathan Lovejoy

# Christ Asleep at the Tomb

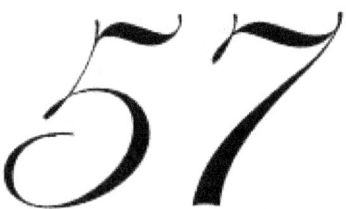

*Bury me not in a shallow grave*

*Bury me wide and deep*

*For if thou hast not drained my blood*

*I'm coming for you in the midst of a tortured sleep*

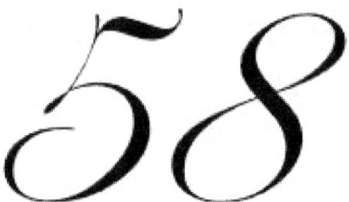

$\mathcal{I}$wake up under the icy blanket of cold premonition, with the distinct and grainy taste of dirt in my mouth. In the haze of sleep come and gone, I look up in time to see her standing over me with something small and black in her hand, but for the life of me, my mind will not process it for what it is. Even when she says to me— *"you are an abomination unto God. I cannot allow you to live..."*

And in the pain of bewilderment, my mind focuses me into lightning clarity of her purpose, though I cannot understand why it must be. As if she is suddenly moving in slow motion, I turn away as she is raising the *pistol* at my head, and as I prepare myself to flee, I feel a flash of light beyond agony explode all around me in a burst of sound, and the world I know is
suddenly pitch black and void.

Somewhere in the blackness of this betrayal, I see Christ asleep at the tomb. This, after the Resurrection from the dead. The crimson of his garment is the red of Redemption, and the cerulean crossover fabric is the blue of God's Creation. Who would know or imagine, that the first thing the Lord did upon conquering death, was to take a nap in the land of the living! Yes, he would be physically exhausted, I suppose, for he was not in a coma in the tomb!

*Just push up until you feel the cold,* I hear a voice say, as the figure of the sleeping Christ begins to fade, and I am aware of myself in a swoon such as has never been, as if Creation itself were spinning, to where I know my only hope for a reprieve is to push and claw my way up through this membrane of pressure I feel pressing down on me. I am suddenly at one with this purpose, until I feel as though I am climbing sold rock, with easy places to grip and pull myself through the spinning dark, where it is impossible to draw a deep breath as I claw my way upward.

Then suddenly, I feel my hand surrounded by icy air, which rushes the breath of life to my body, and I am told to *grab the edge and pull yourself up*, which I do with desperation, until I feel this air hard upon my face in the cold and dark, and the black void around me vanishes into a haze of winter gray and white.

As I struggle to breathe through the pain that throbs my skull, my eyes are kissed by the flakes of new falling snow, and I am aware of the house in the land of the living, and the snows that drift again from these skies of latter day discontent. *There are none righteous,* the voice says to me. *No, not one.*

No, Mother. I am not a zombie.

I am your Daughter.

And vampires are not created.

We are born.

# 59

*The Sugar Plum Fairy dances a twilight dream*

*Across the theatre of my mind*

*On the eve of the Second Coming of Jesus Christ*

*In the snow field of love and grief sublime*

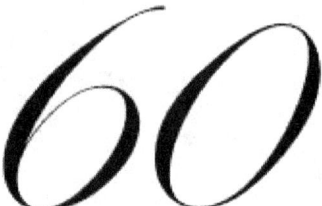

*I*n the warm safety of her country home, in the aftermath of trauma, the beautiful woman showers away the dirt of her calling. Breathing the soapy cleanliness of renewal, relishing the feel of the waters of her sanctification, caressing every inch of her big breasted body. Feeling the return of piety of her spirit, and the superiority of spiritual complacency. *Yes, I did the right thing*, she believes, having one minute swam the waters of debauchery with her daughter, then the next minute cuckolding her unto death with the firing of a pistol. *It was the only way to stop her,* she thinks, *it has to end.*

The beautiful woman soaps her gigantic bosoms for the last time, then lets the water caress them clean, turning the shower off, stepping out into the chilly bathroom air, regretting having not brought in the electric heater this time. But truthfully, whose mind would not be distracted, when their muscles are freshly ached with the digging of their daughter's grave.

In her robe of plush, snow white modesty, she runs the hairdryer for as long as it takes, until every strand of silken, brunette beauty is again fluffy and long, falling about her shoulders and the length of her back.

*It's a good thing I shot her*, she thinks. *Stabbing her definitely wouldn't have worked...*

Thoughts of chocolate bars, Mountain Dews and movies begin to torment the Greenwood mind, calling her away from the beauty she sees in the mirror, past the canopy bed and new white linen, past Bouguereau's *Little Thief* who mocks her in the hall, down the stairs to the kitchen, to where the six-packs of sugar drugs labeled Baby Ruths wait to be devoured. A dozen bite sized fixes of these things will do her body some—

At the moment of her greatest tranquility, the kitchen window frame crashes inward, killing her mood in a shower of glass and brackish noise across the kitchen. A scream for the ages is formed inside her body, but is held in by the shock of pure terror, when she sees a brunette woman in like manner as herself—in long, black hair and white cotton gown stained in filth and blood, with an expression of pure rage and evil—crawl in through the shattered space of a window frame, causing the beautiful woman to run with all her

might towards the stairs, to the safety of her pistol, hidden somewhere in the upper room.

In the outstretched arms of nightmare and legend, she runs in full, bouncing speed to the stairs, looking only toward the top of them to the hall, knowing that whatever hope she has left lies somewhere just beyond her vision. She takes each step in athletic fury, with the fullest speed and intent of purpose, making it to the top of the stairs at last, turning the corner toward the fortress of her upper room.

But the first step of her futility is cut off in mid stride by the grip of strength unbridled, causing her to scream and lose her balance, falling hard in her plush robe to the hardwood floor. She feels the grainy, gravelly grip of Hell upon her ankles, flipping over in time to see the pale, dirt stained hands of certain death begin to claw their way up from her legs to the rest of her body, gazing into the whitened eyes of evil incarnate, with sharp pointed truth gleaming in white inside her open mouth.

The woman is suddenly frozen underneath the clawing female form, who bears the face of angelic beauty in rage, with the feel and the stench of the grave on her skin. The beautiful woman is frozen on her back on the floor, with only the power to scream to the heavens, as the beautiful, filthy thing hisses in the agony of instinct, lowering its head to the woman's neck in full purpose of intent, burying its teeth deep into the woman's skin, holding itself there, listening to the woman scream a death scream, and feeling the life begin to flow rapidly from every inch of her body.

Jonathan Lovejoy

# As the Pink of

# Strawberries

# 61

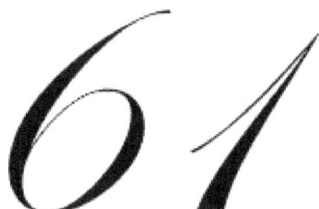

e snows of mankind's discontent continue to fall, passed from the winter and far into spring. This is not a spring of renewal, but where the cold memory of lost Love must go on, in the tragedy of man and womankind's fallen condition.

I languish in the back field of my country refuge, gazing across the snow covered landscape, beyond the place where my mother is buried. Every drop of her life was drained and stored. The taste of her blood is sweet like the juice of the grape.

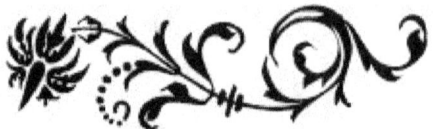

Most wounds of this kind would have exited, the doctor said. The bullet lodged in your brain against the other side of your skull. It is a miracle. It is me.

Every so often, the milk I drink is colored as the pink of strawberries. The essence of my mother's life when I drink to Anya's memory.

On the edge of this uncertain future, I turn away from the grieving winter landscape, walking casually through the flakes of falling snow, into my refuge of country isolation. On the prairie touched by endtime loneliness, and the pain of grief and winter white.

ABOUT THE AUTHOR

Jonathan Lovejoy is a graduate of the University of North Carolina at Greensboro, with a B.A. in Religious Studies, and a graduate of Liberty University with an M.A. in Theological Studies. Divorced after 24 years of marriage, he is a graduate of Grand Canyon University with a Master of Divinity. He currently lives in Mesa, Arizona.

For more info on the author's life and career, visit jonathanlovejoy.com

www.ingramcontent.com/pod-product-compliance
Lightning Source LLC
Chambersburg PA
CBHW051243260626
47162CB00002B/586